tales from the

Hills & Hollers

tales from the

Hills & Hollers

Arlen Davidian

Tate Publishing & Enterprises

Published by Tate Publishing & Enterprises, LLC
127 E. Trade Center Terrace | Mustang, Oklahoma 73064 USA
1.888.361.9473 | www.tatepublishing.com

Tate Publishing is committed to excellence in the publishing industry. The company reflects the philosophy established by the founders, based on Psalm 68:11,
"The Lord gave the word and great was the company of those who published it."

Published in the United States of America
ISBN: 978-1-61739-690-8
1. Fiction; Short Stories (single author)
2. Fiction; General
11.01.26

Dedication

Dedicated to my wife, Debbie, and all those whose
stories have enhanced my appreciation of the contri-
butions from the people in Mid-America.

Acknowledgments

To all my friends who gave their time
to help make this work complete.

Table of Contents

Introduction

" The truth is where you find it," a friend told me when I was just a teenager. After having moved to the hills here in Arkansas, I began to realize that there is a lot of truth in these hills, and you don't have to go looking too far.

There are legends and stories and yarns and sayings and beliefs and omens and, finally, truths that might not meet the criteria as evidence in a court of law. Nevertheless, they are often truths that you will find nowhere else except in these hills and hollers of Mid-America. Some of the truths defy all the rules and laws of physics and chemistry and every other aspect of known science. Yet the belief is so strong that there is no doubt that this too can become a form of truth in itself because much of what we accept as truth is really no more than a profound willingness to believe.

Are these stories that have been told to me unique only to the hills of Mid-America? Absolutely not. Yet out of the hills come great truths that can form a window into this small piece of Americana and in the end become a part of that great puzzle that makes up the greatest nation on earth.

Are these stories and yarns all true?

Well now, that's pushing a button that becomes personal. These stories are all from the mouths of people I know or sometimes from strangers who have spent a few minutes of their time to share a glimpse from the panorama of their lives. There have been people with whom I have talked that have said little but have shared worlds of wisdom. And there are those who have said a lot but really have little to say. Yet from each comes a piece that fits somewhere in the puzzle that makes up this vast and diverse land.

Some of these stories have been told in great detail. Those I have tried to relate in their purest form. Others have been given in bits and pieces that I have had to expand and mold in such a way as to make a coherent story that relates what the teller has tried to pass on. In the end they are stories that defy any challenge of dissection because from within each tale comes a speck of truth as bold and strong as the people who tell them. These are the people whose bloodlines have populated Middle America—Flyover Country, if you will. From their rugged individualism come these stories whose foundations are grounded in the truth.

Gas Gallon Gamble

Shifting nervously, the man squatting close against the side of a pickup whipped around at the muffled click as a bullet slid into the chamber and the breech closed. Willam watched as the man stared into blackness in his direction. The outline of the man's ears and the fuzzy curvature of the scraggly beard were silhouetted in a distant yard light near the house.

Wincing, Willam rolled onto his belly and eased the rifle to his shoulder. Resting the barrel on the bumper of an old car that had sunk into the earth under a huge oak tree. He slowly brought his eye up to the scope and found the crosshairs in the weak light. Wrapping his finger around the trigger seemed to take half the night as he peered into the shadowed face staring right into the crosshairs. His finger pressed lightly against the steel grooves, and his heart began to race.

Gently now, Willam whispered in his mind. He added just a little more pressure, knowing the exact amount it would take to send a bullet hurtling toward its target fifty yards away. He knew how it would sound. He knew how it would feel. It would feel good to send a message through these hills that he'd had enough. He worked hard for the gas he put in his vehicles, and for weeks now it had been disappearing at the will of some unknown thief.

The seconds slipped by, and Willam's heart began to slow. *There's plenty of time to get this critter,* he thought, letting his hand relax on the walnut stock.

The man worked with a hose running from the spout of his gas tank to a three-gallon can sitting on the ground. He shifted on his haunches and raised the end of the hose high into the air letting the last drops run out. Again Willam's finger rubbed the trigger, and his heart began pounding. He shifted slightly and pulled the crosshairs to the man's chest, his finger pulling slowly against the steel.

The thief rocked back on his heels and tightened the cap on the can, then turned into the light. Willam's breath caught, and he clenched his teeth. In the lesser part of a second, he realized he was about to send the neighbor's fourteen-year-old son into eternity. He cursed to himself and held the gun steady.

"The little varmint," Willam said in a whisper. "Steals everything in sight, and now he's getting my gas too. The kid's trash. I'm an old man; he even steals from me." He watched as the thief pushed the full can to the side and slid another shorter can into its place. His face flushed with anger as he realized the little thug was even stealing the can he'd carried in the back of that pickup since he bought it new eleven years ago. His eyes blurred and his heart raced. He pulled tighter against the curve of the trigger knowing the moment when fire and thunder would explode from the cold steel of the barrel.

Willam had lived in these hills for the better part of his life. It seemed that in the last few years, the laws were no longer there to help him. It wasn't fair. He had worked for what he had gotten. When he had caught the neighbors butchering one of his best calves, the sheriff had come out and talked to them but said there was nothing that could be done. It was too late. He couldn't prove to whom the calf belonged.

Two years before, his shop had been raided and most of the tools were stolen. Again the sheriff said he was very sorry but insisted he couldn't make a case even though some of his tools showed up in a garage sale in town and the evidence pointed to his neighbor. Then last year a patch of marijuana was found in the ravine up behind his house. He knew this discovery could be traced directly to the neighbor's kid, but instead, he handed a thousand dollars to an attorney and spent three weeks in the prosecutor's office convincing him that even though the patch was on his land, it didn't belong to him.

When Willam's gas started disappearing two months earlier, he didn't even call the sheriff. This time he would send a lesson into the hills that would remind would-be thieves to think before they took what wasn't theirs. He had fretted for many nights about the gas. If only Elly were still here, she would know what to do. Last Spring she had passed away, and since then he didn't handle things too well. He knew that any solution would have to be found without help from the law. He was sure that Elly would approve if she were still alive.

This was the third night that Willam had lain in the frozen dirt in front of the old car. His chance had come. He closed his eyes and wiped away the cold sweat with the grimy wool sleeve of his coat. It seemed like only a second had passed, but a picture was forming in his mind.

Willam had worked since he was just a boy. He had saved his money in a cigar box under the bed, waiting until he found the right deal on a car of his own. When he saw the '29 Ford pickup on a trip to Fayetteville with his father, he knew that it had to be his. He watched from the front seat of the family sedan as they slowly drove by the lot where it sat.

"That's the one I want, Papa," he said pointing to the black pickup with shiny, green fenders. Willam's father slammed on the brakes and pulled to the curb. They sat looking for a few moments then Papa eased the car down the narrow drive and into the lot. His father walked around the pickup, kicking the tires. He knelt beside the left front tire, which had gone flat. Taking out his knife, he marked the tread with his thumbnail and then ran his hand over the top as if he could somehow converse with the aging rubber.

"Tire's rotten," he said quietly as a man in blue jean coveralls walked over to where they were standing.

"Nice truck," the man said holding out his hand to Papa. "Needs a good home 's all." He spat on the ground. "Was owned by old man Simpson over in Farmington. Never took it off the farm. Didn't want to part with it but wanted a truck I had, so now I got to get rid of this 'n."

"Can you fire it up?" said Papa.

"Runs like a railroad watch, I tell ya. Got many a mile left in her, she does," said the man tilting his head toward the hood.

So Papa and the man struck a deal.

Willam remembered how proud he was when he and Papa caught the bus into town the next day and drove the pickup home. From that day, he never went anywhere alone. He made any excuse to go riding in the country with the back loaded with his friends screaming and yelling at any and all who might be in sight. He never had to worry about gasoline because, wanting to be a part of the gang, his friends chipped in and kept him supplied knowing the alternative was to walk wherever they wanted to go.

There were always girls who were glad to be a part of the good time. Seldom had Willam gone anywhere without one of his girl friends snuggled close in the front seat. Being one of the few kids in town to own a vehicle instantly transformed him into a celebrity.

It was on one of these excursions that Willam picked up Elly and her sister Lida. He loaded a basket with a picnic lunch they had prepared in the back, and the trio went by to pick up Billy who was leaning against his mailbox beside the road to Devil's Den. The four laughed and talked in the crowded space of the front seat as Willam guided the Ford down the dusty road to the Den.

It was well after midnight when the four left the Den. The lights of the old Ford shone on the moon-lit dust of the road as they rode through the woods toward home. They were easing into a sharp turn and began climbing up a long hill when the engine sputtered, then caught, then sputtered again, and died. Willam tried the starter, but the engine wouldn't start. He yanked open the door and stomped across the road, then came back and leaned his head on his arm against the top of the door.

"Outta gas," he sighed. "Thought I had enough to get around." He and Billy discussed the situation, then decided that rather than make the girls walk the four miles into town, they'd leave them and try to find some gas at old man Harvey's place just at the bottom of the hill.

When the pair reached the driveway at the Harvey ranch, they walked quietly up the grass in the middle of the drive. The moon was out, but it was dark among the trees. A dog barked as they sneaked into the yard and stood beside a tree to get a look at where they were likely to find some gasoline.

"In the shed," Billy whispered. The dog was on the front porch and began growling with his teeth bared. "Come on. We can find something by the tractor. Got to have some gas somewhere." Billy motioned, then hunkered down and bolted for the corner of the shed. The dog spun around on the porch and began barking again.

Willam and Billy stood in the moonlight, pressed against the wall at the end of the open shed. When the dog stopped barking, they slipped around the corner into the darkness. Once inside, they felt their way toward the outline of the tractor at the other end. As their eyes adjusted to the dim light of the moon shining through an opening in the back wall, they found a can beside the tractor. Willam twisted off the lid and smelled.

"It's gas," he whispered into Billy's ear. "Must be a gallon or more. Let's take it and get out of here." He started moving around the back of the tractor being careful to stay inside the line of darkness, then stood beside a post and looked around to see if Billy was following.

"Be sure to put the can back when you're done." A strong male voice seemed to slash though the screen of an open window at the end of the house, a calm husky voice that tore at the quiet of the moonlit yard.

Willam could still feel the yelp that escaped his throat and the surge of power that poured into his legs. He could feel the weight of the can of gas as his arm flew skyward, and he bolted into a run out of the shed and down the steep incline of the drive. When he reached the main road, he stopped, and there was Billy right on his heels. He stood hunched over trying to catch his breath when he realized that he was still holding the can of gas in his hand. He couldn't talk but kept gasping for air.

"Come on. Let's get out of here." Billy was pulling on Willam's arm and dragging him up the road toward the stalled pickup. When they had poured the gas into the tank, they stood and looked at each other in the moonlight. Then without saying another word, they walked back down the road and to the top of the drive. Willam sat the can down beside an oak tree at the edge of the yard without moving into the light. He stood for a moment looking at the house to see if there was any sign of life.

The two boys walked back to the pickup and, without saying a word, got in and started the engine. For the rest of the trip home no one talked. The girls sat silently, and the boys let them wonder about what happened while getting the can of gas.

Willam snapped back to the task at hand. His trigger finger was sweating, and his eyes blurred as he watched through the scope. The boy at the side of his pickup once again slid the hose from the tank on the side of his pickup and drained the remnants of gas into the can. He closed the lid and stood up. Willam followed him with the crosshairs steady on the boy's heart. The boy stooped down and picked up the cans and turned to walk down the drive.

Willam's hand tightened on the stock of the rifle, then relaxed. He watched as the boy stepped out of the shadows and into the light. His hand began to shake, and a tear rolled down his cheek. He let the barrel of the rifle slide from its rest on the bumper.

"Be sure to put the can back when you're done," Willam said in a husky voice. He laid his head on his arm and pondered the picture of a boy with two cans of gas flung high in the air as he fled into the night.

Diablo

Diablo was a horse with one cockeye. When you looked at him face to face, he would lower his head and stare up slightly with a look that made you understand that he was just a little nuts and not about to conform with any training regimen that normal human beings had devised. He was known around the country as a devil horse that couldn't be broke. Not one of his five previous owners had ridden him down before. And now he was in Dub's pasture. Dub loved to watch the beautiful paint wander about the pasture grazing at will among his cows keeping the best grass for himself. The devil horse was a gift, and Dub determined to let the young stallion spend his years grazing and watching through his unbalanced eyes the few onlookers who happened by.

Dub was leaning across the fence watching Diablo munch on a bucket of oats he had slid under the bottom rail of the corral. He loved to watch the magnificent horse that came to the corral each morning to get his private fare. He gingerly reached through the fence to scratch an ear, but Diablo laid back his ears and backed just out of reach of the friendly hand that wanted so much to say, "You can trust me." There was no trust to be had, and for more than a year, Dub had not been able to rub the soft velvet nose of the wary horse.

Dub was working in the barn when he felt the presence of a young boy standing in the door.

"What kin I do for ya, boy?" Dub asked, standing his pitchfork against the wall.

"Need some work," the boy said putting a long strand of straw back in his mouth.

Dub looked at the outline of the slender black silhouette closing the space between darkness and the blazing light of an early spring day.

"Don't have nothin' t'day. Might try back when the first hay comes in. 'Bout a week." Dub took a can of saddle soap off a shelf and began rubbing it into the dry leather of a halter that hung stiffly on a peg jutting out from the wall.

"You got Diablo," the boy said stepping into the dark corridor of the barn.

Dub jerked his head up and stared momentarily at the slight figure. He squinted into the brilliant light streaming through the open door. As he approached, Dub recognized him as the kid from a group of wandering Indians who holed up down in the canyon at the back of his place each winter.

"What about Diablo?" Dub leaned forward to look into the young face.

"I kin break that horse." The boy kicked the soft dirt on the floor of the barn with his scuffed and tattered boot.

"That horse'll kill ya. He's not all there, you know." Dub walked to the door and stepped into the sun. He stared across the fence at the beautiful creature with his head stuck in the bucket of oats. "That horse'll kill ya," he repeated looking over his shoulder at the boy who had followed him into the sunlight.

"I kin break that horse. Ain't no horse I cain't break." The boy moved to the fence and rested his chin on his arms that were folded along the middle rail.

"Tell ya what"—Dub stepped alongside the boy— "what's your name, boy?"

"Standing Tall, but they just call me Tall when I go to school."

"How old are you, Tall? Mighty young takin' on a project like this." Dub's eyes scanned the slight figure of the boy.

"Be twelve this next spring." Tall stood up straight to prove his full stature.

"Tell ya what, Tall," Dub repeated, "give ya ten bucks if you can break that horse. But I ain't responsible if ya get hurt, ya know."

"I ain't gettin' hurt, sir. Ain't no horse I cain't break." Tall eased his hand toward Diablo through the slats on the fence.

Diablo eyed the hand but didn't lift his head from the bucket.

Tall withdrew his hand and watched without moving another muscle.

"There's a saddle in the barn and a blanket and bridle. Just make sure you put 'em back like ya found 'em." Dub turned to walk toward the house.

"Don't need 'em," said Tall quietly without moving from where he stood carefully watching every move of Diablo's ears and the shift in his eyes.

Dub stood at the kitchen window watching the boy at the fence. Diablo finished the oats and sniffed the ground looking for the last flake that may have fallen from the bucket. He nudged the bucket with his nose, toppling it over and rolling it toward the fence. His eyes never left the boy standing at the fence, and the eyes of the motionless boy never left the face of the horse.

Dub had spent the day working around the place always keeping a wary eye on the boy who had taken on this impossible task. He had expected him to throw a rope on the horse and snub him to the rope-worn snubbing post in the center of the corral so he could get a saddle on him. But the boy hadn't moved from his position leaning against the fence until Diablo had been satisfied there were no more oats laying about and had wandered through the open gate and into the pasture.

Tall pulled the brim of his hat down over his eyes and climbed to the top rail of the fence at the far side of the corral. He wrapped his arm around a post and sat motionless watching the paint as he inched from one clump of grass to the next.

It was late in the afternoon when a cloud moved across the valley and rain fell on the dry grass. Diablo hadn't slowed his grazing nearby, inching ever closer to where the boy sat, still hugging the post.

When dusk began to settle in, Tall got down from his perch and walked to the back of the barn and picked up a bundle and a rifle he had left there when he arrived early in the morning.

"Not goin' ta eat?" Dub asked, walking toward the barn.

"Got some bread in my pack. Still got work to do with that horse. Sure is a beaut, Mr. Dub. Make ya a fine horse when I get him broke."

Tall threw his bundle over the fence. He carefully leaned his rifle against a rail and slipped his fragile body to the other side. Picking up his belongings, he walked out into the pasture where he leaned his rifle against a huge oak tree and sat in the damp grass.

Darkness had drawn its cloak about the pasture as Dub stared out the window above the kitchen sink. He watched the figure of the boy hunkered against a tree staring into the flames of a small fire that flickered in the night.

It was after midnight when Dub climbed the stairs to his bedroom. He pulled back the curtain just slightly

and peered across the pasture where he had last seen
Tall hunkered against the tree. The coals of the fire
cast a dim light on the boy curled up under a blanket.
On the crest of the hill not far away stood a lone horse.
His head was down. His back leg was relaxed, the toe
of his hoof rested lightly in the dampened earth.

Dub stretched and yawned, then threw back the
blankets and sat on the edge of the bed. He stretched
again, then pushed himself to his feet and walked to
the window. The sun was driving the darkness up in a
line above the horizon. He stared toward the tree. The
boy and the horse were gone.

It was Sunday morning, and the wife would be taking the kids to church. Dub had plenty to do about
the farm. He had Saturdays and Sundays to get the
hard work done before he had to drive the battered
'39 Ford pickup to his job running an old dozer building a county road through the steep countryside of the
Ozarks. At the end of each day, he parked the dozer and
drove home. The old pickup rattled and coughed as it
clambered over the rocks and ruts of the driveway that
wound its way up the steep grade to his house. Each
afternoon he pulled up in front of the barn and sat carefully scanning the pasture looking for any sign of the
Indian boy and the devil horse. Tuesday evening he had
saddled up the sorrel mare and had ridden across the
pasture looking for any signs of the pair. There wasn't

a broken branch or hoof print or crushed mat of grass that gave any indication they had been nearby.

By Thursday evening Dub began to worry. He saddled up the mare and rode over the hill and down into the canyon at the back of his place. It was dark under the cover of the dense forest when he rode into the Indian camp. He slid down and dropped the reins on the ground, then walked to the edge of the fire where several men were staring at the flickering flames.

"How kin I help ya, Mr. Dub?" asked an old Indian, his wrinkled face accentuated by the light of the fire.

"Worried about that boy." Dub sat on the ground when the old man motioned him to join them by the fire.

"No worry. Standing Tall takes care of hisself. No worry." The man didn't look up from the fire. "He be back three, maybe four days. Standing Tall takes care of hisself."

Dub sat for a long while sharing the fire with his elusive neighbors. They were never a bother on his place. They hunted deer and rabbits and coons, but never in the years they had wintered in the canyon had they been known to steal or to kill his cattle. By early spring, they were usually gone, but this year they had stayed on longer than usual.

"Two weeks, maybe, we work in Kansas," the old man explained. "We have good winter. Lots of pelts for trade this spring." It was dark when Dub mounted up and pushed the mare past the two dilapidated Model A trucks parked at the edge of the clearing where the

Indians had made camp. He gave the mare her head and let her make her way up the steep canyon and back to the barn.

Sunday afternoon when Dub's wife returned from church, Dub was standing at the fence staring out across the pasture. A horse and rider were keeping to the shadows along the edge of the trees. Dub watched, wary of strangers who were known to bring ill will to the local farmers and to leave with things not their own. He eased to the barn and lifted his rifle from the pegs on the wall inside the tack room. When he stepped back out into the light, Tall was standing inside the corral holding a rope, which he had tied around Diablo's neck and looped over his nose forming a makeshift hackamore.

Dub stared at the pair in disbelief.

"He broke?" Dub asked.

"Yep." Tall slipped the rope off Diablo's nose and untied the rope from his neck.

"Better get him a bucket of oats. I'll go get your ten bucks."

Dub went to the house and came back with a crisp ten-dollar bill.

"Naw," said Tall. "Cain't take no money, Mr. Dub. Ain't right. He's a friend." Tall picked up his pack and slung it over his shoulder by its rope tie. He picked up his rifle and started to walk off toward the gate of the corral.

"You can have the horse. You earned it." Dub stood staring at the slight magical figure of the Indian boy walking away.

Tall turned and walked back. He reached up and scratched Diablo behind the ear. Diablo lifted his head out of the bucket and nuzzled Tall in the chest, pushing him back playfully. He reached out with his lip and pulled gently on a snap on Tall's shirt and nickered shaking his head.

"Cain't take him with me. Got work comin' up in Kansas." Tall leaned against the powerful shoulder of the young stallion.

"Then he'll be here when you come back this fall. You can be sure he's yours." Dub reached through the rails of the fence. Diablo looked for a moment at the outstretched hand, then eased up and let the fingers gently rub his nose.

"I just got to know your secret," Dub said running his fingers over Diablo's ears.

"Just like people," Tall said, kicking the toe of his boot into the dirt. "They got to learn ta trust ya. Ya eat, ya sleep, and ya live with 'em, and after a while you become friends. They're just like people. They got ta learn ta trust ya," he repeated. "Got ta go, Mr. Dub. Leavin' for Kansas in the morning. See ya in October, Mr. Dub."

Dub watched Tall move into the shadows of the woods along the pasture then disappear. He patted

Diablo on the side of the neck and lifted his chin with his other hand and stared into his eyes.

"It's not really you that is cockeyed lookin' out," Dub said. "Maybe it's us that's got a cockeyed view lookin' in."

A Throne a King
Does Not Make

Alex sat rocking back and forth on the seat of the commode. Hitchhiking to school carrying a white porcelain commode was going to be more than just a day's work. It was hot and the school dormitory was still fifteen miles away. Cars flashed past without slowing or seeming to notice the forlorn figure perched on the glaring white fixture planted firmly in the gravel at the side of the road.

A bright red pickup slowed and then stopped about one hundred feet down the road from where Alex sat. He stood up and lifted the commode awkwardly against his chest, the tank wrapped firmly under his arm, and walked briskly toward the waiting vehicle. He could see the driver looking into the side mirror as he approached, and just when he was about to reach for the handle on the tailgate, the driver spun away, spraying gravel into Alex's face. The four boys in the front laughed and yelled as they sped away.

Down the road the pickup skidded to a stop then backed up. The boy on the passenger side jumped out and came back to where Alex was standing. He dropped the tailgate and lifted the toilet into the back.

"Get in," the stranger said. "You must be from that boarding school up on the hill. We're going right by there on our way to the lake."

Earlier that morning Alex couldn't contain his glee, knowing that Jack, his neighbor across the hall, would be reaching the bottom of the stairs any minute and bursting through the front doors of the dorm on his way to class. Jack's exit would bring him right beneath Alex's window making a perfect target for him to drop the cherry bomb he held lightly in his hand.

Alex stretched out his window and peered over the sill to survey the sidewalk three stories below. He could see the shadow of a figure as it passed through the door and down the steps behind a giant Sycamore tree that blocked his view. He struck a match and lit the fuse, timing the path of the figure as it would emerge into sight and within easy throwing distance from the window above.

The fuse sizzled, and the figure emerged. To Alex's horror, from behind the tree stepped the chancellor of the school. With an audible gulp and a giant leap,

Alex charged to the bathroom and tossed the lit cherry bomb into the commode and pulled the handle. There was a reverberating thud followed by a blast of porcelain chunks intermingling in a sheet of water spreading in an ever-expanding circle around the gaping hole where a toilet had stood. Water from the broken line that attached to the shattered tank gushed in a plume of spray above Alex's head, filling the room and drenching everything in the crowded space.

In a panic, Alex dropped to his knees. Pushing his face into the spray, he reached out and turned off the valve, bringing the plume of water collapsing down upon him.

It seemed like an hour had passed before Alex lifted himself from the puddle of water that covered the floor of his bathroom. He pushed a foot forward in the mess feeling for sharp pieces of the shattered porcelain with his bare feet. Slowly he transferred his weight and then pulled the other foot forward reaching with his toes for the carpet just beyond the bathroom door. Water squished up between his toes as his weight pushed into the dense nap of the rug that covered the floor.

Classes had begun long ago when Alex finished cleaning up the mess and put on his clothes. He had used every towel, every spare sheet, and had even dug into his drawer to use all his T-shirts to soak up the water and keep it from seeping into the ceiling of the room below.

When Alex eased through the window to descend the fire escape at the end of the hall, he stood for a moment beside a bush at the end of the building. He had avoided the ever-present monitor sitting in the office at the entrance to the dorm. He surveyed the landscape to see if the dean's car was still in its place just outside the front door. The dean had not left, so he walked briskly around the back of the dorm and into the woods.

By the time Alex reached the highway into town, it was almost noon. The sun was hot, and his skin burned from the tension of the escapade of the morning. He stuck out his thumb and a beat up pickup with a cattle rack on the back pulled along side. A farmer heading to the auction at the stockyard greeted him and offered to take him to the hardware store in town where he could purchase a replacement for the shattered commode.

It took Alex's last cent to purchase the new por-celain throne. The owner of the store explained each step necessary to install the fixture. He helped assem-ble the tank and the bowl and install the valve inside. Patiently he discussed the need to make sure the wax ring was seated properly and that the stool must be affixed securely to make sure there would be no leaks. When Alex lifted his burden and walked outside, the owner stood in the middle of the sidewalk in front of the store and watched as Alex lugged the new com-mode to the corner and stuck out his thumb.

Alex had waited at the corner for half an hour, but no one offered him a ride. It was getting late, and he knew that classes would be getting out soon. The football coach would be sending someone to his room to check on the reason for his absence when he didn't show up for practice, and the dean would be informed that he had not gone to any of his classes. Time was running out so he began to walk. It was more than a mile to the highway, and he could make only a hundred feet or so before he had to set the toilet on the ground and rest. When he arrived at the highway, he set the porcelain bus in the gravel under a tree and sat down to rest. He waited with his chin in his hand and his thumb out until the pickup load of boys gave him a ride back to school.

The instructions that the storeowner had given were perfect. Alex was pleased with himself as he opened the valve and watched the water rise in the tank. He checked for leaks, then sat with his head in his hands on the shiny new seat and dozed.

Alex jumped with a start when there was a knock on the door. He grabbed the pile of soaked towels and sheets and T-shirts and shoved them under his bed. The damp circle on the carpet stared back at him as he opened the door and gazed into the face of the dean.

"May I come in?" he asked.

"Uh, sure." Alex opened the door wide and watched as the dean entered the room and sat in the chair by the window. He didn't seem to notice the damp circle or the pile of damp towels under the bed. He just leaned back and clasped his hands behind his head and looked around the room.

"Haven't been up here for several weeks, so I thought I'd drop by and see how you are doing."

"Uh, yeah. Sure," Alex stammered looking furtively at the dark circle forming around the pile under the bed.

"Everything okay? Keeping up with your classes and all?" The dean stood up and walked to the door. He looked down at the dark ring on the carpet.

"Yeah, keeping up okay," Alex answered.

"Okay then. Go to the laundry. Mrs. Simpson has a pile of towels waiting that you can use to dry out this carpet. She'll get all this mess washed up for you also. And make sure that new toilet doesn't leak. Mr. Black will be by later to check it out." The Dean smiled and stepped into the hall.

"And by the way," the Dean said sticking his head back through the door, "over at the girls' dorm they're saying hitchhiking with your own throne, a king does not make. It just ain't cool!"

Repo Man

I met Stan on the plane while returning to Arkansas from California. We chatted and exchanged bits and pieces of our interests, ideas on the political scene, and the weather. He was an officer in a large Southern California bank and was fascinated when he discovered that I was from Arkansas.

"You know," he said, "I'd never really known what it was like outside of big cities until one day in a weekly meeting with the officers we were discussing a loan that had gone bad."

Stan had arranged a loan for a trucking firm whose main office was in Southern California. When he presented the package to the committee, everything had been right between the lines and the numbers couldn't have been more perfect. The president of the firm wrote a check for the down payments on the six new semi-tractors and refrigerated trailers that would be delivered to the firm's yard in Arkansas.

When the first payment came due and then became delinquent, Stan was not concerned until he called the local office and discovered the phone had been disconnected. He checked the number and tried again. He was not mistaken.

That afternoon, Stan drove to the address given on the application only to discover that the "office" was in an alley and up a rickety set of stairs behind a dilapidated grocery store in a seedy section of town. The door stood open and was hanging by one hinge, and a window was broken out. Papers lay scattered over the floor. On a battered desk an ancient phone sat looking lonely among a few papers held down by the weight of the instrument.

Stan shuffled through the scattered papers looking for anything that might give the surreal picture a sense of realism. There was nothing, not even a letterhead that related to the trucking firm that had been presented with every "i" dotted and every "t" crossed. Every balance sheet had been in perfect order and every tax form and a full credit report had completed a picture of exceptional bookkeeping acumen that traced the management of a well-run company.

Stan returned to his office without stopping for lunch and slumped down in the high-backed leather chair at his desk.

"How could I have been so stupid?" he said out loud, slamming his fist down on the walnut top of his massive desk. He had no idea how to spin this personal example of bad judgment at the committee meeting scheduled to assemble early in the morning.

Stan entered the room and looked down the length of the conference table at Mr. Matthews, the bank president, who didn't look up from a stack of papers.

"Have a seat, Stan," said Mr. Matthews still pawing through the heap.

Stan sat while the other members of the committee took their places and sat in silence waiting.

"Seems we have a problem, Stan." Mr. Matthews looked over the top of his glasses. "Have any information to add to what we have recently learned about trucking?"

Stan followed a snicker down the table to a man who looked too young to be out of diapers.

"Seems that all the information presented by these guys was bogus." Stan hesitated and then went on to explain the situation at the office he had found during yesterday's lunch break.

"What do you propose we do to recapture at least some of the losses we are apparently about to sustain?" asked Mr. Matthews, removing his glasses and setting them on the table. He folded his hands across the stack of papers and waited.

"Well"—Stan cleared his throat—"well, I have contacted a firm out of Oklahoma City that is in the business of repossessing trucks and heavy equipment. They say they can get the equipment and re-sell it for an eighteen percent commission plus costs."

"Have you checked to see if they really have an office?" Mr. Matthews smiled tightly, shoving his glasses back on his face.

There was another snicker from the boy at the far end of the table.

"Well, sir." Stan picked up the one piece of paper he had brought to the office and flipped it over nervously to look at the back, which was totally blank. Turning it back over, he scanned down the page to a paragraph entitled "References."

"They appear to be a reputable firm. They had been in business for three generations and have a clientele list that includes some large truck dealers and banks, including Ford Motor Credit. I called on several references, and they pan out with good recommendations."

Stan spent another few minutes explaining the information he had on the trucking firm to whom the loan was given. He had called the office in Arkansas but was told that the owner was out and would not be back until the first of next week.

The committee put the case in Stan's hands and asked him to report at the next meeting.

The repo firm had been contacted and retained to get the equipment back. They said it could take several months but should be nothing more than a routine repo situation. They'd find the equipment and do all the preparations necessary to get the best price possible. Stan estimated that the bank would net about fifty cents on the dollar and suggested that this was probably the best they could expect according to the firm in Oklahoma City.

Three months passed. Each time Stan contacted the repo firm, they assured him that all was moving according to plan and that it would be just a short time until all the equipment would be in a storage yard and ready to put at auction. Time was dragging on, and Stan was getting nervous. He was under pressure from his supervisor who had to report to the president, and Stan didn't have any more answers.

It was late in the afternoon when Stan got a call from Oklahoma City. The president of the repo company himself was calling to inform him that they were not interested in pursuing the contract on the trucks and that he was sending a letter to confirm his unwillingness to be further involved.

Stan was stunned. He had another committee meeting the next morning. He was already without any further solutions to the dilemma. When he left the office that night, it was after ten o'clock, and the streets were quiet. He knew that there was no one else to whom he could turn and that his job depended on no other human being but himself.

It was early when Stan returned to the office. He was printing out the last report he had prepared when his secretary entered and reminded him that he had a meeting with the committee in five minutes. When he entered the room, he threw his shoulders back and walked briskly to his chair near the head of the table.

"Where do we stand with regards to the trucks that seem to be plying the highways and byways of this country without the weight of any financial obligation to this bank?" Mr. Matthews was unusually sarcastic.

"Sir," Stan stood up and handed a piece of paper to Mr. Matthews, then passed a copy to everyone at the table. "It seems that the repo firm wishes to no longer be involved with this situation. They have given no explanation other than they are just out. I have only one other idea to suggest and that is that I fly back to Arkansas, find the trucks, and get them back into our possession."

"Just when do you propose to do this?" Mr. Matthews sat up and leaned forward in his chair.

"I can leave Monday morning." Stan laid out the plan outlined on the sheet of paper. He went through all the expenses, airline tickets, fees for service of process, food, motels, and the cost of hiring drivers.

The committee accepted his plan, and Mr. Matthews patted Stan on the back as they were leaving the room. "Keep me posted, Stan. You have some guts to suggest this plan."

Stan rented a car in Fort Smith and drove east on Interstate 40. He turned north on a state highway that made county roads in California look like freeways. The road wound its way into the steep mountains of the Ozarks, then into a valley, which cradled a tiny town. A gas station at the edge of town looked abandoned when he pulled the shiny blue sedan alongside the pump. He stepped out and began replenishing the depleted supply of fuel in his tank.

"Help ya, sir?" The man that approached from inside the broken down building that housed a garage and what served as an office, tugged on the strap of his coveralls that clung to the edge of his slumping shoulder. The other strap draped in a long loop at his side, and the bib flopped over exposing the gray hair on his pinched chest.

"Looking for this trucking firm," Stan said pulling a piece of paper out of his pocket and showing it to the attendant.

The man pulled a crooked pair of glasses out of his bib pocket and shoved them onto his face with the palm of his hand.

"Ain't never heard a such."

"They're supposed to have an office here in town." Stan felt a wave of apprehension sweep over him, and his face became instantly hot. "They gave this as their address. Would this be a phone number you'd find in this area?"

A battered red pickup pulled up on the other side of the pump, and three bearded men got out. One fiddled with the pump while another lifted the hood and nosed around checking the oil. He jumped back when he opened the radiator cap and scalding water shot skyward filling the air with the sweet stench of rusty anti-freeze. The third man leaned against the back of the pickup drinking a beer and stared at Stan when he reached for his wallet.

"Might be. Sen'teen dollars for the gas. Phone at the cafe." The man pointed across the street.

"Take credit cards?" Stan asked flipping through a stack of cards displayed in his wallet.

"He don't take no plastic stuff," the man leaning against the back of his pickup said while rolling a toothpick back and forth across his teeth with his tongue.

Stan looked at the attendant quizzically.

"Gotta have money."

Stan pulled out a twenty and handed it to the attendant who pulled a sweaty wad of crumpled bills out of his pocket and handed him three ones.

"Need a receipt," Stan said apprehensively as another pickup with four boys jammed in the front seat pulled in close behind him. The outline of a rifle in the back window silhouetted against the bright afternoon sky made Stan nervous.

The attendant pulled a damp and tattered receipt pad from his other pocket and handed it to Stan. "Here, put whatcha want." The man handed Stan the pad and a stubby pencil that had been hidden in the dense hair that covered his ear.

All three men that had arrived in the pickup on the other side of the pump were leaning against the side of the pickup staring at Stan as he wrote out a receipt on the stained pad, which had no letterhead at the top.

"What's the name of this place?" Stan looked at the attendant and waited for an answer.

"It's Jeb's," One of the men leaning against the pickup answered.

"What's the hold up?" The boy driving the pickup behind Stan's car leaned out the window and banged on the side of the door with the palm of his hand.

Stan didn't answer. He folded the bills and stuffed them into his pocket. He looked back at the four boys in the pickup and shook his head, then got into his car. As Stan drove forward toward the street, a car pulled in blocking his exit. He waited as the car pulled ahead pushing a tire over the curb and onto the sidewalk, leaving Stan just enough room to maneuver into the street.

The cafe was abandoned when Stan pushed open the door, which hit a cowbell hanging on a wire to herald his arrival. There was a row of padded bar stools that lined a counter extending the length of one wall. Several tables were scattered across a black-and-white tile floor, which created a checkered pattern that hurt his eyes as they fought to adjust to the contrast of the bright sun he left in the street.

"Hello, ma'am," Stan said as a huge woman came from the kitchen. Her graying hair was pulled back in a bun that tugged at the back of her head.

The woman wiped her hands on her apron and stared without answering.

"May I use your phone?" Stan pointed at the ancient black instrument sitting beside a sink sagging from its mount on the wall.

"For customers only." The woman continued to stare.

"I'll have a coke then." Stan pulled the three bills from his pocket and thumbed them into a fan.

The woman pulled a glass from under the counter and slammed it on the linoleum that graced the top of the counter.

"Pepsi only," the woman said. She slid the glass under a spigot and pulled down hard on the handle.

The cowbell above the door clattered, and the three bearded men from the gas station down the street pushed through the door.

The woman slid the glass across the counter and snatched a dollar bill from the fan in Stan's hand. Then without saying a word she stuffed the bill into a shirt pocket under the bib on her apron and set the phone on the counter.

"No long distance," she said without moving from her position where she stared across the counter.

The cowbell clanged, and Stan looked toward the door. The sunlight blinded him momentarily as the four boys jostled each other as they moseyed across the room and tussled noisily for a position at one of the tables.

The dial on the ancient phone was worn, and the numbers were hard to decipher in the dim light. Stan pulled the phone toward him and started dialing, checking each number as he twisted the dial. The woman was watching every move of his fingers as they spun through the numbers written on the piece of paper in his other hand.

The scratchy ringing in the receiver when Stan finished dialing broke through the harsh silence as he waited for an answer. In the dingy light of the room, he became aware that every table had become occupied. At the other end of the counter the three bearded men leaned over and stared at the scowling old woman standing with her feet firmly planted and her hands resting on her ample hips. "I'm sorry, that number is no longer in service." Stan jumped at the scratchy voice that came over the phone. He sat the receiver back on the hook then picked it up again and started to redial.

"Number's no good," said the old woman. "Ain't been nobody there for mor'n eight months."

"Do you know where I can find this man?" Stan asked holding the piece of paper toward the woman with his thumb under the name.

"Been dead for better'n three year," the woman answered without looking at the name.

Stan stood frozen in the dim light of the café, staring across the counter at the woman.

"I just talked to him a few days ago," Stan protested.

"Not him. Been dead for mor'n three year. Talked to one of his boys maybe." The woman picked up the phone and set it back in its place by the sink, then moved down the counter in front of the three bearded men. "Gonna order sumpthin' or just standin' here to make more nuisance?"

"Ma'am, do you know where I can find his sons?" Stan asked leaning slightly forward over the counter.

"Nope. Moved away when their daddy died. The rent don't get paid when you boys don't buy nuthin'," the woman said to the men at the counter without a skip in her train of thought.

"I need to find one of these boys," Stan insisted.

"Said she can't help ya." The man closest to Stan leaned back on his elbow and sat on the edge of a barstool. "Moved away. Ain't never seen 'em since."

The musty air in the café suddenly became thick with tension. Silence began to build in the room like the pressure on a dam, when the light dimmed as the sun outside moved behind a cloud. Stan slid his glass of Pepsi toward him nervously as he scanned the room, which had filled with staring faces of men who occupied every table. He pushed the glass back and walked into the street.

"So did the bank ever get those trucks back?" I asked when Stan stopped talking and stared out the window into a thick layer of clouds far below us.

"Oh," Stan snapped back and pulled a magazine from the pocket in back of the seat. "Nope. The bank never figured out what happened to 'em. Just disappeared. Poof. Gone." He laughed out loud and stared back out the window.

There was a long silence as I waited for Stan to finish the saga that seemed to die with his blue sedan parked at the curb in a tiny town in Arkansas.

"Did the bank just write off the loans?" I felt desperate for an ending to this story.

"So where you at with all this now?" I finally said pushing for more answers.

"Well," Stan said pulling a pillow from his lap and stuffing it behind his head. "Banks have a hard time with the reality of broken promises that have no solution. And the boys in Arkansas? You might say they were having a hard time dealing with no work for the trucks that, uh, you might say, just disappeared." He chuckled and looked down at his watch. "The bankers were glad to stick me with the bad paper and titles to the missing trucks in exchange for my measly severance pay," he continued. It all worked like magic with my retirement. So, now I'm going back there to fix up my café and gas station. Gotta cater to my employees. You know, the bearded boys and their four cousins who are now driving my disappearing trucks. The old lady who refuses to put on a new apron will still be standing guard over the phone. The man at the station? That pencil is still stuck behind his ear." He leaned back, closed his eyes and grinned.

Just Five Hundred Bucks

Habib heard the coins clank on the counter and turned as the door slammed behind a customer who had just paid for a beer. He slid the coins into the drawer and turned back to the wall, tears running down his cheeks.

The door opened again. Habib wiped his eyes and turned around, his dark face silhouetted against the white background of the wall behind him. He laid the phone on the shelf and looked up at the men on the other side of the counter.

"Mr. Singh?"

"Yes," answered Habib. "May I help you?"

"I'm with the ABC and am here to read you your rights." The man pulled a wallet from inside his coat pocket. He flipped it open to expose a gold badge, then flipped it shut in the same motion. "You've just sold a beer to a minor, and it is our duty to arrest you."

Habib's knees got weak, and he slumped into his chair. He never sold liquor to minors. Even the old lady down the street became incensed when she first came in and he made her show her ID. "Why, son, I'm old enough to be your grandmother." He remembered the feeling of the heat that rushed into his face when the reality of her age sank in. He carded everybody until he came to know them well. Now he was accused of selling to a minor.

The officer took out a leather folder and ceremoniously opened it and began to write.

"We are not going to take you in, but you are going to need to appear before the judge on Wednesday morning." The officer filled out the information, then looked at the liquor license on the wall to get the information needed to complete the ticket. He handed it across the counter and pointed to an X at the bottom with his pen.

"Sign here," he said. "You are not admitting guilt, but you are only agreeing to appear on the specified date."

Habib had just stepped through the door that morning when the phone rang. He picked it up and heard the voice of his sobbing mother.

"Your cousin in Detroit was killed in the riots last night," she sobbed. "He was just trying to defend his store. Someone came in and robbed him then shot him in the chest before they ran out."

Habib faced the wall leaning his head on his arm. He felt weak, and tears were rolling down his cheeks. This was the cousin that had been his best friend. They had gone everywhere together. When they parted and his cousin moved to America, they vowed to meet again when he settled in and could bring Habib there too.

In America, Habib saved his money while working for his cousin in Detroit. When an opportunity arose to buy a small store in Arkansas, Habib went to his cousin for advice, and when he had moved to Arkansas, it was this cousin that had turned his own store over to his sister and had spent a week helping Habib set up the new store here on the corner. He could not picture a world without his best friend.

Distressed by the call and the sobs of his mother, his mind racing to take in the reality of this loss, Habib didn't hear the door open, and he didn't hear the customer come to the counter. He only heard the clank of coins on the counter and saw the back of the man as he went out the door. He was not aware that this was just a boy not yet seventeen who had been sent to set him up and buy a beer. And now he was staring down at the ticket he was being asked to sign.

This is America, and this should not be happening, he thought as he scratched his name on the bottom of the page. *In the old country, yes, but not here in America.*

Habib was early when he appeared in the courtroom. He waited patiently, watching as the proceedings moved through the docket. When his name was called, he stepped to the podium and waited.

"How do you plead?" asked the judge.

"I guess I am guilty, but I'd like to explain."

"Are you pleading guilty or not guilty?" asked the judge looking over his glasses.

"I guess I'll plead guilty, but I'd—"

"Sit over there. We'll hear your explanation after the others are heard. Next."

It was another hour when Habib was asked to step up and explain his situation. He told his story, stumbling occasionally over words that were complicated by the heavy accent of his broken English.

The judge leaned back easily in his chair as he listened to Habib's story. When he was finished, he leaned forward and looked over his glasses.

"I'm really sorry for the loss you have sustained, but I am still going to have to fine you five hundred dollars. In sympathy to your situation though, I would recommend that you change your plea to not guilty and get yourself an attorney to help you in this difficult circumstance. Would you like to consider this change of plea?" The judge waited for an answer.

The room seemed stuffy and hot, and the silence pressed down as Habib tried to put all that was happening into a perspective that he could understand.

"I guess that's what I'll do," Habib mumbled quietly.

The attorney listened to the story, then assured Habib that this was a "slam dunk." This case will get thrown out in a heartbeat when the judge hears the story.

When Habib met his attorney on the day of the trial, he was nervous, but the attorney patted him on the shoulder and told him there was absolutely nothing to worry about. This case would not go anywhere. The prosecuting attorney was just doing his job when he refused to drop the charges and forced them to trial.

The proceedings seemed to drag on as the judge moved through the docket. When Habib's name was called, his attorney stood and said he represented Mr. Singh and that he would like to proceed to trial.

"Just exactly what is the situation in this case?" asked the judge, having no recollection of the story Habib had related a few weeks before. "Can't we wrap this matter up quickly?"

The attorney approached the bench and told the story. He explained that Habib's policy was to card everyone, leaving no possibility that liquor would be sold to a minor from his store.

The judge listened, then looked at Habib and offered his condolences. He dropped his gavel on the desk and declared the case dismissed.

As they walked out the door, a great burden seemed to lift from Habib's shoulders. His attorney put his arm around him and congratulated himself for getting the case dismissed. He told him again how sorry he was about his cousin and that if he ever needed anything more, not to hesitate to call.

"It's been a pleasure helping you through this difficult time, and it's only going to cost you five hundred bucks!" said the attorney pulling on his coat.

A Thin Veneer

"It seems, Mr. Johnson, that we've met before in circumstances that demanded we not meet again." The judge looked over his glasses into the dark eyes and black skin of the man standing before him, then shuffled through a sheaf of papers stacked on his desk. "That'll be sixty days and five hundred dollars. Now, Mr. Johnson, before the bailiff takes you to your home for the next sixty days, I recommend that you reflect on our past conversation and work on building a little more durable veneer that will bring you up to speed on what civilization demands of its citizens."

The judge slammed his gavel down on the desk and leaned back in his chair, then looked over at his clerk. "Who's next?" he asked.

The week before, Louis had stood before this same judge pleading for leniency from the court for his misbehavior. That day had started out normal, a little work and a short dog of wine. The cops had been normal, even tempered and courteous. The jail cell was normal, chilly and damp. Many times over the years he had been subjected to the same routine. But a week ago, he had a girlfriend waiting, and he had plans for a little time spent in the company of his new friend. Fate that evening had leaned a bit in the wrong direction. Having had just a little too much to drink and driving just a little too slow, he had been spotted by a roving cop and hauled in to jail.

Louis knew the routine. Cop a plea, and try to get the court's attention. He knew if he could just get back on the street, the old man at the foundry would let him earn enough money to take his girl on a couple more dates. Even the court proceedings seemed normal except the bailiff had led him into the courtroom without handcuffs or shackles. He sat in the "cage" in the corner of the courtroom sandwiched between several unfortunates who were there on similar charges and with similar stories.

The clerk made the roll call. After each name he looked up long enough to determine if the defendant was indeed present. Louis' name was last. He slid down in his seat on the wooden bench and rested his chin on his chest preparing psychologically for a long day in court.

"Please rise," the bailiff said coming to his feet as the judge entered.

The judge looked over the docket and looked at the pile of folders on the clerk's desk. He leaned forward and peered over the rail that surrounded his desk at the front of the courtroom.

"Looks as though we have a long day of it, so let's not dally over the details of these proceedings. This is an arraignment only. You will stand right here in front of me when your name is called. You will then enter your plea. That plea will be either 'guilty' or 'not guilty.' There will be some of you that for some unknown reason will feel compelled to explain your behavior. If you so wish, tell me your plea, then add that you would like to explain. When all have been heard, you can try to tell me a story that I've never heard, thus convincing me that you should have some special treatment due to your extraordinary circumstances."

The judge leaned back in his chair.

"Who's first?" he asked, waiting for the clerk to read a name.

Louis had counted the names when the roll call was made, and by lunchtime the judge had not heard even the first half of those on the docket. When his name came up, Louis entered a plea of guilty but with an explanation. The judge gave him the same funny look and a slight shake of his head that he had given seven others who had made the same plea before him, then asked him to wait in order to have his explanation heard.

Yeah, right, Louis said to himself as he sat back down on the hard bench. *Just where does the judge think I might be going? Back to bed?*

This was a tough one today. Usually Louis didn't care if he had to spend a few days as a guest of the city. Meals weren't so hot, the cells were cold, and the company was way below compatible. But sleep was abundant and risk and responsibility didn't exist. He could just lie in his bunk, rest, read a few tattered magazines, and prepare a story for his pushover boss so he could get his job back.

Louis tried to read the judge's mood after each fantastic story he heard. He was sitting straight up now putting together a whopper of his own, knowing that this one the judge had never had the occasion to hear. Then the second man who got up to tell his story slouched up in front of the judge.

"And what would you like to tell me?" asked the judge.

"Well, sir, me and my girl were just sitting home drinking, and we ran out of beer. I just drove down to the liquor store to get another six-pack, and this cop come out of nowhere and nailed me. Your honor, honest, all I wanted to do was get another beer."

Rain on it, Louis thought, *almost what I was about to say.*

The judge closed his eyes and dropped his chin to his chest to hide a gaping grin. The attorneys slumping down in their chairs in the front row stopped their whispering and suddenly looked up to hear the verdict.

"Thirty days, and two hundred dollars," the judge said, shaking his head in disbelief.

The third man limped to the front of the bench. He smiled with his hands folded in front of him and waited for the judge to speak.

The judge looked over the rail. "And you're accused of being drunk and disorderly."

"Well, sir"—The man hesitated, then continued when the judge nodded—"it just wasn't fair. I was upstairs minding my own business, and those dummies, er, that is, those people downstairs kept banging on the ceiling. All I did was go down there to make them stop, and a fight broke out."

"And?" The judge leaned hard on his hand and waited.

"And what?" the man asked.

"And what were you doing upstairs that might have made your neighbors downstairs bang on the ceiling?" The judge was thumbing through some papers while he talked.

"Well, I just don't understand. All I was doing was tuning up the engine for my boat."

"Thirty days," said the judge shaking his head while reading some notes on a pad. "Next."

Twice Louis had figured out a good story, but both times some guy before him used his line and got thirty days. He was getting desperate. He had a date with a beautiful woman. This wasn't the time to go to jail.

When Louis' name was called, he stood up straight and walked briskly toward the bench. He looked at the attorneys lined up in the front row. One was sleeping, another was writing on one of those legal pads, and two others were whispering to each other. He straightened his shirt lapel and stood erect waiting for the judge to speak.

"Okay, what's your story? It's late, and I want to go home, Mr. Johnson." The judge smiled as he looked over the rail into Louis' black face. He leaned forward folding his hands across the stack of papers and waited.

"Your Honor, I'd like to plead for the clemency of this court. You see, due to my ancestral background, I have obtained only a thin veneer of civilization."

The judge yanked himself upright, slapped his hands down hard on the desk without a hint of a smile and stared. The attorneys stopped their whispering, and the one who slept sat bolt upright in his chair. The bailiff, who had been leaning lazily against the rail of the witness stand, snapped to attention, and the clerk stopped writing in the middle of a sentence to listen.

"Just how would you like to explain this personal deficiency you described?" The corners of the judge's mouth turned up ever so slightly, and his eyes brightened in anticipation.

"You see, Your Honor, my people have been exposed to civilization for a mere two hundred years. When you compare this to the thousands of years the great civilizations of the European or the oriental nations have had to develop their practiced behavior, this is nothing more than a thin veneer of civilization that my people have been able to acquire."

The judge sat back in his chair and held his chin in his hand as he shook his head. A grin spread across his face, then he began to laugh. He leaned forward and folded his hands across the stack of papers and looked Louis in the eyes.

"Mr. Johnson," he said with a chuckle. "I thought I had heard every story known to mankind, but in my twenty-nine years on the bench, this one is a first. Now, it is late, and I am tired, but I will leave this courtroom with my heart a bit lighter because of your story. But if I ever see you in my courtroom again, you had better be able to demonstrate to me that this thin veneer has been thickened exponentially. Go home now and have a good evening, Mr. Johnson."

Rag-Tag Platoon

Tharin took a stick and pushed it down along the inside of the thin leather of his upper boot and vigorously drew it back and forth until it drew blood, but the itch just got worse. In desperation he rolled over in the dry grass and dragged the boot off his foot. A tick had crawled under his tattered sock that slid down under his heel. The dark brown body proudly displayed the familiar white dot that seemed to stare up at its victim like a taunting beam of a light that said, "Here I am, you sucker. Take me, kill me if you wish, but my legacy will linger on in an oozing red weal that will itch for days."

Tharin scrambled to slide his boot back on and jumped to his feet. In one motion, he snatched up his rifle and snapped to attention.

"All right, you raggedy 'uns. Let's get a move on. There's a war to be fought. Them Yanks is movin' north outa Loosiana, and it's our'n opportunity to kick some Yanks about 'fore they move too far into Mozurri."

Captain Wilson Harlow's gravelly voice grated against everything for which Tharin stood. He was young and handsome, which made Tharin a little uneasy. The captain's wiry strength and good looks made Tharin feel like his hatred for this leader was not wasted.

Everybody knew that Captain Wilson Harlow did it; they were just too scared to talk about it. Wilson was mean. He was a bully who would use his powerful physique to intimidate and browbeat those who served under his command. Everyone knew that even his kids and his wife hated him, but in the end they had nowhere to run.

When the war between the states broke out, Wilson was one of the first to grab up his rifle and join the Confederacy. War suited him well. He could bellow out commands, and men by the hundreds would jump to his beck and call. Now he was leading a relentless drive of more than three hundred and fifty irregulars, a rag-tag troop at best, toward the Arkansas-Missouri line to link up with the Confederate army in a desperate attempt stop the progress of the Union forces moving north.

It's just too bad I know too much about this rat! Tharin thought as he did a right face on command. He picked up the cadence as his platoon dragged themselves through the dust and rocks of the wagon road that snaked its way along the edge of a steep bluff above Pitcher Creek.

Tharin broke cadence and kicked one foot in front of the other as he lost awareness of the trudging troop headed for Prairie Grove. His rifle hung at the end of his arm as if tied to his hand with a lanyard, and each step dragged a tiny puff of dust up around his ankles. He was aware of the rising humidity, and his ears burned, a sure sign of impending rain. He looked up at the sky and felt the change in temperature as a cold front from the northwest moved across the dry grass of cleared spaces through which this motley outfit marched as they cut west toward a road that led to Fayetteville.

The humidity became oppressive as the warm air from the gulf was driven upward by the mass of cold air hugging the ground from the north. Clouds were rolling in bringing shade to the blistered ground parched by days without rain. These forces in nature's own war zone were moving into a desperate battle as if to portend another conflict between the Confederate South and the Union North. Huge drops of rain began to fall. Each drop drove a tiny crater in the thick dust amidst the sparse blades of grass. The drop shimmied for part of a second, then disappeared in a dark splotch leaving its lifeblood in the desperate soil.

Arkansas had been bitterly divided over the issue of slavery. The state lay in the midst of the controversy, and the blood of its citizens had been spilled like the rain falling on the parched October soil. The plantation mentality of the southern part of the state had finally overpowered the few that held out in the north-west, and on May 6, 1861, cessation was approved, and Arkansas joined the Confederate States of America. Each conflict drove another nail in the coffin of the Confederacy as General Winfield Scott's "Anaconda Plan," which called for the long-term strangulation of the south, began to take its toll. The struggle for the Northwestern Mountains of Arkansas was a desperate attempt to regain some control of Missouri, the only slave state north of the 36th parallel.

Tharin looked up into the sky and licked the drops of rain that fell on his parched lips. He marched mind-lessly on, stumbling occasionally when his feet no lon-ger being guided by his up-lifted eyes caught a rock or a stray clump of grass. He pushed back his hat when he heard the command to break ranks at the edge of the road that led from Sunset to Fayetteville. He knew the territory well. Many a day he had spent courting his girl at Sunset Community. Many a night he had spent lying in these woods fighting the hatred he had for his archenemy, Wilson Harlow, who had made it his life's work to divert the affection of his sweetheart.

When Daisy and Tharin had married, it seemed to make the ground for Wilson's advances more fertile. When children came, Wilson did not let up. He lurked nearby. He was there when Tharin was working at the mill. He showed up at the house to chat with Tharin when he knew that Tharin would be gone. He met his kids after school and told them how pretty his girls were or how tough his boys were. He was always there, always intimidating, always ready to leave his own wife and family if only Daisy would forsake her own.

Days of marching toward a place of conflict with a foe he didn't know had not softened the hatred Tharin had for the enemy he did know. When he was forced to join the Confederate Army he did not expect to be placed under the command of an officer he hated so much. For half a year now he and the men in his company had been driven by their relentless captain who used intimidation and humiliation like a whip to keep his forces moving.

The dry layer of dust pressing down on hardened ruts in the road to Fayetteville began to sag with the endless soaking by water being squeezed from the sky. Three hundred men slogged through the deepening mud before Tharin's platoon set their boots into the quagmire. When the sun was just above the trees, the call to bivouac brought strained relief to the tired troops. A fence of twisted wire whose barbs were rusted and broken guarded a vast open field where camp was being set up.

Tharin leaned his rifle against a locust post, pushed a strand of wire down, and then squeezed his body through. He picked up his rifle and stared angrily at the captain who was leaning against a cannon standing idly in the middle of the road while he talked with his First Lieutenant.

Wilson pushed his hat back and wiped his forehead with a gloved hand, then walked across the road and leaned his rifle against the wires of the fence. Bending low, he pushed down on a strand of wire and kicked his leg through. As he slid his body between the taut wires, the rifle began to slide toward him. Transfixed by the evolving danger, he let go of the wire with his gloved hand to grab the falling rifle, allowing the wire to snap up and tangle in the crotch of his breaches. Jerking frantically sideways to wrench himself free of the grasp of the steel barbs, he slipped forward and stared directly into the open bore of the rifle. The rifle slid toward him, guided by the wires by which it was supported. An explosion brought instant silence to the hubbub of three hundred and fifty soldiers settling in for the evening meal. Three hundred and fifty pairs of eyes turned to stare at the exploding face of the captain who stood bent down snagged by the barbs on a wire fence. Blood spurted from a gaping wound just above the bridge of his nose. His body, frozen in space and time, slowly leaned away from the fence. His knee buckled as he crumpled to the ground. The troops stared in horror at the lifeless body with one leg still caught in the barbs of a wire fence. Three hundred and fifty pairs of eyes turned to stare at Tharin who nonchalantly pushed his hat back with his forearm and wiped the sweat dripping into his eyes. He settled his rifle loosely across his knees and leaned back against the tree and closed his eyes. In seconds three hundred and fifty men busied themselves with their evening meal.

Early in 1863, Little Rock and Fort Smith fell under the control of the Union forces. Tharin went to his commanding officer and requested that he be allowed to return home. It had been more than a year since he left Daisy and the kids.

The boys were playing in the yard when Tharin leaned his rifle against the gate post in front of the white house overlooking the railroad station in the little town of Winslow. He clapped his hands, and the boys ran and leapt into his arms. He squeezed them until they squealed for him to let go. Martin grabbed his daddy's hat, and Ray picked up the rifle and then ran up the path and onto the front porch.

"You know better than to run with that rifle," Tharin scolded just as Annie, the hired maid stepped through the door to see what the ruckus was about.

"How's my Daisy?" Tharin asked, slapping his hands down lightly on her shoulders. "Ain't no change, Mr. Tharin." Annie's black face was drawn wanting desperately to be able to give a better answer. "She jus' sit there a starin' an' a rockin' like usual."

It was dark in the room when Tharin entered. Daisy was sitting where Tharin had left her more than a year before. It seemed that she hadn't moved or even changed position. Her hair was pulled back and wrapped tight in a bun, and her gingham dress was freshly washed and ironed.

"I been keepin' your sweetheart fixed up and ready, knowin' you'd be returnin' one day." Annie brushed Tharin aside and pushed back a lock of Daisy's hair that had fallen across her eyes. "She jus' be sittin' an' a rockin', Mr. Tharin. Jus' a sittin' an' a rockin'." Annie's voice trailed off in quiet desperation.

Annie pulled back the drape on the window that overlooked the railroad station and watched as the train that had brought Tharin home pulled away from the platform.

"I be leavin' you two alone, Mr. Tharin," Annie said, pulling the door shut as she stepped into the hall.

Tharin stood at the window staring as the train disappeared behind the cut through the mountain that led to the tunnel.

"He's dead, Daisy." Tharin didn't turn away from the window. "You don't have to worry about him any more. He's dead. Shot between the eyes, he was."

It had been seven years since Tharin had quit his job at the mill and had taken a position as headmaster at the school. He loved to come home after a day with all "his" kids and tell Daisy about the progress he had made with his problem students and how much his best learners had done.

School was winding down when Tharin walked up the steps and onto the front porch. There was a crushing silence. The usual sound of the boys tussling on the living room floor or in the backyard was not there. The clatter of dishes in the kitchen was not there. The rustle of Daisy's dress as she rushed down the hall to meet him was not there. Just silence.

The boys were standing just inside the library door when Tharin entered. In a second, his whole world came crashing down around him as he stared down at Daisy curled up on the floor by the shelf filled with her favorite books. He fell to his knees and drew her toward him trying to fix the full picture of what happened in his mind. Daisy pulled her knees up to her chest and covered her face with her arms. She was crying softly, wrapped in the strength of her tortured body.

Tharin lifted Daisy into his arms. The two girls sat motionless on the couch, and the boys just stood watching as Tharin carried his sweetheart into the hall and up the stairs to their bedroom. He laid her on the bed and began removing her bloodstained dress.

"Who did this to you?" Tharin asked, pushing the words through his clenched teeth.

Daisy rolled onto her side and pulled her knees tight against her chest like a little child. Her body shook, and she whimpered incoherently. Tharin washed the blood from her battered face and chest and then slipped her into a fresh nightgown. He bent down and placed a kiss on her swollen cheek, then pulled the covers up and left the room.

The sheriff had come to the house and tried to talk with Daisy. She only sat in her rocker and stared out the window and rocked back and forth. He asked a few questions of Tharin, then left saying he'd be back in touch.

Weeks went by, and the sheriff never got back. When Tharin went to his office, the answer was always the same, "It's under investigation."

Daisy wouldn't talk. The kids spent each afternoon sitting near her, chattering and talking about the day at school or the garden or the Sunday church picnic, but Daisy still wouldn't talk.

When war between the states had broken out at Fort Sumpter, Tharin continued teaching though he had lost many of his older students who had joined to fight the incursion of the Union forces into what was deemed the sovereignty of the Confederate States of America. Each afternoon he would sit on the couch in the library and read to Daisy who just stared out the window and rocked in her chair in cadence with the tidal ebb and flow of her breathing. He talked with her and discussed what he read, but she did not respond.

The flood of volunteers was not sufficient to meet the need for troops to sustain a resistance strong enough to beat back the Union troops moving north after their victory at New Orleans. Inflation had put the cost of a Confederate dollar's worth of flour at sometimes more that ninety dollars. Farms and plantations were being ransacked, homes were burned, and skirmishes popped up everywhere. In a desperate struggle to augment the Confederate forces, troops were conscripted from every town and village.

Tharin walked into the library and knelt at Daisy's feet. He rested his head on her knees and openly cried. "I've got to leave you for a while," he finally said. "Annie's going to take care of you and the kids. She'll be here till I get back." He stood up and wiped his face with a handkerchief. Daisy didn't respond but just rocked and stared. Tharin walked into the street and boarded the train to Fort Smith.

Walking away that day had torn away a part of Tharin's life. He stood at the window and thought back over the year and the hatred that had brewed and the torment he had felt when he was assigned to the command of Captain Wilson Harlow. He smiled, and his eyes glowed with a dim light ignited by a secret that he was sure many others knew. He turned from the window and knelt on the hardwood floor at Daisy's feet. He took her hands in his and drew them to his face.

"He's dead, my love. He'll never bother you again." Tharin looked deep into Daisy's vacant eyes searching for something that said the love of his life was still in there.

"He's dead," Tharin repeated. "Shot between his eyes, and they didn't even check my rifle." He laid his head on her knees and closed his eyes. A hand drew across his face. A warm, gentle, soft hand brushed back the hair from his face. He lifted his head and looked up into the gentle smile and the bright eyes of Daisy who had come back from the dead.

For a Roll of Lifesavers

The headlights dug into the pavement, then shot skyward into the trees as Omar's car bounced over the tracks that crossed the dimly lit road. He drove slowly looking along the broken sidewalks and deteriorating houses that lined the streets. She was here somewhere. Perhaps she was sleeping under a porch or holed up with a friend, but he knew she was here. He felt sick because Pushcart Mary had not come back. Then he whipped his car to the curb and jumped out.

"If you take care of the people in this community, they will take care of you." Habib's words rang in his ears like a drum reminding Omar of his stupidity. "These people are basically honest. They have little money, and they have even less incentive to be productive. But they religiously spend their money here in this store."

Habib had made a tough decision to move back to Detroit when his cousin had been killed in the riots the past summer. His mother needed him. All his cousins, aunts, and uncles, not to mention his own brothers and sisters, needed him. It seemed a natural to move back to Detroit. To confirm his decision, his store on the corner sold just one week after he put it on the market.

Omar, the new owner, was young and enthusiastic. He had lots of ideas that would be able to consume some of the energy that he was willing to expend on this enterprise. A big part of the business that Habib had explained was the line of customers that would be waiting each morning to get their daily fix of alcohol, a quart of milk, or a half dozen eggs. There was an unconventional kinship among the assemblage that met on the sidewalk in front of the store. Each morning, Habib explained, he would open the store at six, and the patiently waiting patrons would enter two at a time. Each would make his rounds, then come by the counter and make arrangements to pay when their next government check would arrive. On the third of each month, the line would be no different except that Omar would need to bring lots of cash to the store to make change for the checks that his customers would bring throughout the day.

"Cash their checks, give them the money, and then hand them their bill. They will each ceremoniously pay their bill; charge another six-pack, a short dog, or a box of biscuit mix; sign their chit; and be back tomorrow. Don't try to be a conscience for your patrons," Habib had carefully explained. "You are providing a service to people whose needs will be fulfilled either by you or by stealing the money to buy it somewhere else. If you work with them and let them run a tab, you will make friends that you never knew could be so loyal. They will protect you. They will guard your interests, they will brag about being your friend, and mostly, they will help you make a profit. In the end you will benefit, the community will benefit, and you will be a benefit to your customers in ways that you may never realize until years later."

Omar listened intently to the philosophy that Habib had developed working with these people for eleven years in this decrepit, deteriorating, dark enclave along the river in Arkansas.

Habib carefully described many of the customers and their individualities. The Man would be there each morning in front of the line. The others knew he was to be at the head of the line. When on one occasion a newcomer showed up and usurped the position, a warning was sent up that he must defer to "The Man." He was always first.

Jackson was sneaky. He was loud and liked to shove and push his weight around. He was tall and slender but commanded the respect of all who gathered each morning in front of the store. His bluster and pomp were well known throughout the community, but deep down, his comrades knew he was a wimp and a thief.

Each morning Jackson came into the store and headed straight to the shelf at the back, took a "short dog" of Thunderbird wine and plunked it on the counter. Under his long coat would be hidden a long neck of Busch beer that played a primary role each morning in the game. Habib had explained to Omar that it would be his duty to point at Jackson's coat nonchalantly and then ring up the long neck along with the short dog without making a big issue of the incident.

"Jackson will give you an 'oh yeah' and put the long neck on the counter explaining that it's for his friend and dutifully sign his chit with a smile and wait for the next morning to try it again.

"About once a month, I kinda forget about the long neck. Jackson thinks he pulled one over on me," Habib explained. "What he doesn't understand is that each morning I make a clear profit on his purchase that pays for that long neck a hundred times a month. But he thinks he's winning the game when he gets one by me, so he comes back each morning to try it again. He's fun to watch. If I go just a little too long before he catches me, he begins to get nervous. He spends just a little longer in the store watching for his opportunity and hoping that maybe I'll make a mistake and let a third person in to divert my attention so he can slide one by. Sometime, somehow, he knows he'll finagle that free beer.

"Now, about Pushcart Mary," Habib explained. "She is a good customer that purchases a six-pack each morning, then a half pint of rum in the afternoon. For the past eleven years she has patiently waited her turn to come to the counter with her six-pack. Then each afternoon she comes to the counter and raises her gnarled finger to point to a bottle of rum on the top shelf behind me. Each time I turn around to reach for the bottle, I see her in the mirror take a roll of lifesavers off the rack and slip it into her pocket. When I ring up the rum, she reaches into her purse and pulls out the cash to pay. Each day I put the money in the drawer and say 'thanks,' but she never responds. When she comes back the next morning, she plunks a six-pack on the counter and sucks noisily on a stolen lifesaver she openly displays between her broken teeth."

Habib smiled as he sat on the stool behind the counter and watched Omar work the register. "For eleven years Pushcart Mary thinks she's been slipping one by, when in reality, I have cultivated a good customer and have made a healthy profit on her business.

"I've got to tell you about Louis," Habib continued. "He's smart, he knows the language, but he loves to fight. Well, that is, people in the community love to pick fights with him. When he was in the army; he claims he was champion in the ring for the Western Division. He says it was a cakewalk until he met the Eastern Division champion for a title match. Louis says he saw the champ, a slovenly hillbilly from West Virginia who slouched about and seemed hardly capable of lifting himself out of the chair in the local bar." Habib chuckled as he related the story.

"Louis was so unconcerned about the upcoming match that he didn't bother to train but spent the week before the bout drinking and chasing around the bar scene. When the day of the fight arrived, he entered the ring eying his opponent slumped in the other corner. When they met at the center of the ring to get the final admonition of good sportsmanship from the referee, the hillbilly dragged himself up and slouched about with his gloves dangling at the end of his arms as if they were weights that kept his scrawny arms from floating in the air. His eyes sagged, and he had trouble holding his chin off his chest. Then the bell rang, and he came off his stool on the tips of his toes. When the round ended, Louis says he sat in his corner stunned at the power of his opponent's punch. For the rest of the fight, Louis worked fervently to stay away from the hillbilly and his terrible punch that he admits produced a clear victory for the hillbilly."

Habib laughed at his own stories. "He'll be in here in about fifteen minutes unless he finds a shack-up for a few days or got into a fight that put him in the hospital or jail. When he returns, he'll give you a full rundown in great detail.

"Louis always pays his bill. He'll go for several weeks at times. When he runs out of money he'll go to work at the local foundry for a few days or weeks. His first paycheck will come here. He'll pay up his bill then charge a couple of short dogs." Omar listened intently trying to absorb the information about each personality as Habib talked.

The door opened, and a tall black man entered with a basketball under his arm. His gray, kinky hair glistened in the sun that filtered through the tinted glass on the door.

"Can you spare a few bucks?" the man asked, setting the basketball on the counter.

Omar looked back at Habib who sat on the stool jammed in the corner.

"Louis, been a couple of days. This is Omar. He'll be taking over as of today." Habib slid off the stool and leaned against the counter. "He's okay," he said looking at Omar.

"When you going to sell me that basketball, Louis?" Habib asked. "I'm going to be going back to Detroit and would sure like to take that ball with me."

"You been trying for eight years to get this ball. The cover's gone, it's out of round, but it brings me luck." Louis draped his huge hand over the ball and lifted if off the counter. He turned it over and gazed at the dark surface, then put it back on the counter. "Nope, this ball stays with me."

"You any good?" asked Omar.

"Some say so. Found my first ball when I was five. From that day a ball was always under my arm or bouncing down the street. When I started school, the teacher tried to take it away. The ball and I went out the door. A truant officer brought me back the next day, and the ball stayed with me. From the day I found that first ball until I got off the bus at Fort Ord, a ball was my companion. It slept with me, it went to school with me, and it went on dates with me. In the end, the

DI at the base won but only after a fight." Louis shook his head sadly. "Nope, the ball stays with me."

"Well, that's my last try. I leave tomorrow." Habib shook his head and laughed.

"Whatcha got?"

Louis leaned back and looked out the door, then slid a small pistol out of his pocket and laid it gently on the counter.

"I need a little cash and a six-pack of Dos Equis. It's the pistol my boss let's me use when I work late at the shop." Louis glanced around nervously. "Thing about this gun, it only shoots cans." He paused waiting for the comment to settle on his audience. "Mexi-cans, Afri-cans, Puerto Ri-cans, Ameri-cans." Louis leaned back on his heels and bellowed at his joke, then suddenly became serious.

"I'll have the cash by Friday. I found this girl that I want to take to dinner tonight."

"He won't tell you how much, but he needs twenty-five." Habib looked at Omar with a smile.

When Louis signed the chit and left, Habib laughed. "I'll call his boss. His boss will come down and pay me the twenty-five bucks and retrieve the pistol with a laugh. He knows Louis will be back to work in a couple of days. His guilt will drive him to really produce for a few days. Then Louis will come in Friday with his check and not another word will be mentioned about the gun. Louis thinks he's putting one over on you knowing that this pistol is only a starter's pistol and isn't worth a buck fifty. It's part of the cycle. In that cycle, you will continue to make a profit because Louis will keep coming back."

Habib sat back on the stool and watched as Omar worked with his patrons. The afternoon sun was pouring through the window that stretched across the front of the store, casting ribbons of shade across lines of shelves like bars on a prison cell. Habib slid off the stool and stretched with a yawn.

"Let's go stand outside and enjoy the day," he said. "Even the outdoors here on the street has a life of its own." Habib walked around the counter and pushed open the door.

Omar slipped his apron over his head and laid it on the counter, then stepped into the sunlight. Habib was standing at the side of the building looking down the alley at a card game in serious progress. Four young men stood at the curb pitching pennies at the wall. They argued and pushed each other in playful bouts of mock pugilism, vying to establish a meaningful pecking order.

"Hey, Mack, Abraham Lincoln died a hundred years ago." Jackson shouted at an old man leaning against the wall.

"Ain't neither." The man pulled a flask of whisky discreetly from under his coat and took a sip. "Rents the apartment back of my house, he does."

"You're nuts, old man."

"Sure enough does," said Mack, slipping the flask to his lips again, then pushed himself from the wall, yanked his hat low over his forehead, and walked with exaggerated briskness down the street.

"Mack's a regular," Habib explained when he and Omar had resumed their positions behind the counter. "He's about the only white guy that comes in here. Nobody knows just how much he's worth, but the rumor is that he owns most of this end of town. It's a mystery whether he really thinks Lincoln rents from him or if that is a subterfuge to divert attention from something else he doesn't want to surface. He buys a bottle of Jack Daniels every day and always pays with one-dollar bills and exact change. He puts the bottle in his coat pocket and sips from a silver flask while he leans against the wall for a couple of hours, then makes that hasty retreat to his house on the corner three blocks down. I tried to raise the price a couple of years ago. He just kept laying the same amount on the counter and walked out. This went on for several months, then one day he came in and pulled a paper bag out of his pocket and spread ninety-three dollars and some cents on the counter. 'Guess you're not going to insist when prices go up, boy. You need to learn that a fair profit is nothing to be ashamed of. This is how much you've lost in just six months.' He pushed the money into a pile and handed me the exact change for his bottle of whiskey at the new price and walked out. He never misses a day, and ever since, he always winks when he comes to the counter."

Habib leaned forward on two legs of the stool to look at the clock and then settled back on all four with a crunch.

"At 4:05 every day, the delivery man pulls up to the back dock and unloads the order I gave him from the day before. Stays pretty much the same each day." Habib reached for a clipboard hanging on a nail behind the counter. "Hasn't changed for years. Best if you have the back door unlocked when he arrives. He can wheel the goods right into the storeroom. If it's locked when he unloads, it'll be up to you to carry the stuff in. Jesse doesn't wait for anybody." Habib handed Omar the keys and walked to the back. He showed Omar how to jiggle the lock just right and then to throw the latch back so he could roll open the door. He stepped from the darkness of the back room into the sunlight and watched as the truck pulled to the curb.

"Never misses and always on time." Habib waited until Jesse came around the back of the truck with his first load and introduced Omar.

"Hard to believe that after all these years you're really movin' on," Jesse said, looking at Habib and shaking Omar's hand. "This man's my best customer on the route. Learn all you can before he leaves."

"If all he says is true, there's a lot of psychology I need to put to work. He has a story for every customer and a warning for at least half." Omar laughed.

Omar tried to help put the things in the cooler, but Jesse wouldn't see of it. "I'll take care of this. You keep your eye on the counter, or I may never get paid."

Omar stepped behind the counter and looked at several stacks of pennies pushed neatly together by the register. "What's this?" he asked looking at Habib.

"That's from David. I swear he waits until I go back to unlock the door until he comes in. He goes to the back and gets a loaf of bread. He's a legend around here at pitching pennies. He pays each day with the pennies he has won. He puts them in neat piles on the counter and walks out. It's almost as if there's a mark where each stack should go. And in every stack not one is ever out of line." Habib shook his head and pushed back on the stool.

"About four years ago, David came in and wandered about from aisle to aisle. When I asked if there was something I could help him find, he just shrugged. I watched him for about fifteen minutes when the delivery truck drove up. I went to the back door, keeping my eye on him the while. When I came back up front, he was gone. About an hour later, Louis walked in leading David by the arm.

"This boy has something to say," Louis said.

"I waited without wanting to break the mood of the occasion.

"David reached into his pocket and pulled out a handful of pennies and dumped them on the counter. Without saying a word, he began to stack them in perfect piles, pushing them together as he completed each one." Habib paused. "You know, it always amazes me just who you find to be your friends. David had never been in before that day. Louis says he's a little retarded but tries to take care of his mother and sisters. Anyway, all he said was, 'Mom needed a loaf of b-b-bread. C-can I go now?' Every day when I go to unlock the back door, he gets his loaf of bread and leaves the money in neat stacks on the counter. You can bank on it."

Habib leaned his head back against the wall.

"Remember I told you that it may take years before you learn of some of the good in the people that may be known as derelicts of society. Every Friday Louis makes the rounds of all the guys on the street and takes up a collection. He and several of his friends come in and make their way up and down the aisles filling two grocery sacks with food. He brings them to the counter and hands me the money he collected to the last cent. The few cents left over from the collection I record right here." Habib leaned forward and pointed to a page in his register of charges. "The extra is applied to the next week's supplies. Well, remember the circles, it begins all over again."

Habib closed his eyes and smiled as he thought about the years he had been working in this forgotten part of town. He thought about the personalities that made up the patronage that had made him a good living for the past eleven years. Many of the forsaken souls he was sure were really angels taking care of God's children who had been crammed into the pit of this dying community.

"Louis would never say what happened to the groceries, so one day I did the unspeakable and closed the store when Louis left carrying a sack of groceries in each arm with his basketball precariously tucked under his chin on top. I followed him for more than a mile until he turned down along the river. He greeted everyone as he walked along and called them by name, knowing he was on a special mission. I waited at the corner trying not to be seen. He cut across a vacant field along the docks and headed toward the bridge. To my amazement, he stood behind the abutment and waited. Behind a broken down fence several children were playing. On the porch, a woman sat in a battered wheel chair. Louis watched for several minutes, then ducked behind the tall grass in the lot next door and disappeared behind the house. When he appeared again, he was bouncing his basketball down the sidewalk in front of the house.

"'Hey, Mrs. McGrath. What a beautiful day,' Louis shouted across the fence, tucking his basketball under his arm and setting the broken gate to the side. He gave each of the kids a hug then sat on the porch at the woman's feet. I couldn't hear what they were saying, but by the look on the woman's face I knew this was a special moment. Then to my greater surprise, David came down the walk with a book in his hand and walked up the steps. Louis jumped up and grabbed him in a bear hug that I began to think would never end."

Habib paused and brushed the hair back from his face.

"I heard David say, 'I-I'm doin' like you said, Mr. Louis. I-I read a book a week, and I-I learn a new word every day, a-and I don't steal no more neither, Mr. Louis.'"

Habib watched Omar working the counter without talking for more than an hour when Pushcart Mary walked in. He slipped down off the stool and walked around the end of the counter and stood looking out between the bars of the front window. This was a moment that he didn't want to interrupt.

"Mary," Habib said, walking back to the counter, "this is Omar. He will be taking over the store. I must go back to Detroit and take care of my family. You know, since my cousin got killed in the riots."

"Why, you be a-leavin' us, Mr. Habib. Won't be the same hereabouts when you ain't here no more." Pushcart Mary shook her head and looked up uncertainly at the bottles of rum high on the shelf above Omar's head. "I want one of them," she said raising her gnarled finger up toward a half pint of rum.

Habib stepped behind the counter and turned his back to Pushcart Mary.

"She gets the half pint of Captain Morgan spiced rum," Habib said, relishing the moment as Pushcart Mary slipped the roll of lifesavers into her pocket while Omar reached up for the prize.

Pushcart Mary took a bill from her purse and laid it on the counter, then put the change back and walked out.

There was a long silence as Omar watched her disappear through the door and down the street. He just stared at the emptiness on the sidewalk outside.

It was after nine when Habib and Omar locked up for the night. Habib stood back and stared at the front of the store dimly gracing the corner in the light of a street lamp. He knew he would miss the store, but family ties created a need he could not resist. The light in his car came on when he pushed the key into the slot, and there on the seat sat a black round object. For several seconds he stood staring, then pulled open the door and peeled back a note taped to Louis's basketball.

"I always told you locking your car was to keep honest people out. Let this ball be a reminder that sometimes people leave with more than they brought, but you, sir, are leaving us far more than you are taking." Habib sat thinking for a few moments, then started the engine and pulled into the vacated street.

Omar parked his car in the lot at the side of the store. He was early for his first day to open his new store alone. Already there was a line of men and women waiting for the doors to open.

The door swung in, and stale air of the captured night filled Omar's lungs. He eased the door closed and eyed the group of patrons that waited for him to invite the first two customers to enter. There at the head of the line was The Man. Jackson leaned against the wall, and Pushcart Mary stood erect in her full shortness clutching her purse under her arm. Omar began to relax as the routine began to unfold, and he became acquainted with each customer that Habib had so carefully described.

The weeks passed, and each time Pushcart Mary reached for the day's roll of lifesavers, Omar felt a twinge of disdain for this blatant theft. The seed began to grow, until one day he snapped.

Omar whirled around when Pushcart Mary reached for the roll of lifesavers and grabbed her arm. He peeled back her fingers and pulled the roll into his palm and put it back on the rack without saying a word. He sat the bottle of rum on the counter and handed her the change.

Seven weeks had passed, and he had not seen nor heard from Pushcart Mary. When he asked his other patrons, they just stared and shrugged. Louis was the only customer that gave him any indication that she was even still in town, but he just said she was being taken care of.

The streets were still dark when he saw her and whipped his car to the curb. She was curled up in her dark blue coat against the hedge that bordered the old Baptist church parking lot. She was ensconced in a stupor imposed by alcohol and clutched a bottle of Captain Morgan spiced rum close to her chest.

Omar knelt down beside the quiet form and put his hand on her shoulder and rolled her face toward him.

"I came to get you Mary," Omar said lifting her into his arms. "You didn't deserve what I gave you, and you don't deserve this."

Pushcart Mary looked up and smiled. She reached out and pulled her wrinkled hand across the stubble on his face. "You be a good man, Mr. Omar. You be a good man. My Louis tell me you be worried. You be a good man, Mr. Omar."

Omar drove silently into the parking lot beside his store. He threw open his door and rushed around the front of his car to open Pushcart Mary's door. He held out his hand to her and helped her to the pavement. Together they walked arm in arm across the lot to the front of the store.

There was a hushed silence along the line of customers who stared as the duo walked up. "The Man," Omar said with a broad smile, "I need your help. You are still The Man, but from now on I want you to make sure Pushcart Mary gets to stand at the head of the line."

The Man thought for a moment, then a big grin spread across his face.

"No sir," he said, "you da man, Mr. Omar." He reached into his pocket and pulled a roll of lifesavers from his pocket. He held them up between his finger and thumb for everyone to see.

"Lifesavers anyone? From now on Pushcart Mary can get her own."

A Long Date

The black limo stopped alongside the steps that led to the front of the girls' sorority and the chauffeur stepped out. He straightened his jacket and walked briskly up the walk and into the lobby.

"Here to meet Miss Jessica Martin," he said to the lady at the desk.

Mike and Hugarte were roommates. They spent little time together in the surroundings of their apartment due to their conflict in schedules, but whenever Hugarte had the opportunity he would ply Mike with questions about the American ritual of "dating." The business of courting was foreign to this student from Ethiopia who was sent to America to get an education and to learn the American ways. When he returned to his homeland, his parents wanted him to be Americanized to the extent that he could run their lumber business the "American Way" and extend their vast wealth throughout the world. Yet clinging to old customs, they had decided that Hugarte was to be subjected to their ancestral customs and forced into a dowry marriage of their choosing.

Mike got back to their room late one night to find Hugarte laying fully dressed on his bed staring at the ceiling. All the lights were on, and his books were scattered across his desk.

"You okay?" Mike asked, setting his books on his bed and hanging his coat in the closet.

"Yeah, but I got this question."

"Let's have it," Mike said, shuffling through a pile of papers on his desk.

"Tell me again how you get a date in this country." Hugarte sat on the edge of his bed dangling his feet above the floor.

"Well!" Mike slid his chair out, kicked his leg over, and sat resting his chin on the high back. "You just walk up to a girl and ask her if she'd like to have dinner with you."

"It's that simple?" Hugarte stared at the ceiling knitting his eyebrows and squinting at the light.

Mike had roomed with Hugarte for three years. He was an exceptional student in the Humanities and Business Administration. Mike's own interests in science and medicine never seemed to interfere with their occasional discussions in the world of international politics and the social conflicts that were brewing in the late sixties in America.

The racial issues of the day never seemed to perturb Hugarte. He was confident, and his self-esteem was always well grounded in the knowledge that his ancestors derived from the royal line of kings and princes in Ethiopia. Then there was the aspect of great wealth, which Mike knew was vast to the extreme, a fact that Hugarte never ever flaunted.

Mike's freshman year was a desperate struggle to stay in college. Money was always an issue. He often washed his clothes by hand in the sink and ate sparingly of the dry, cold cereal he kept in the cupboard of a tiny closet in a room he occupied in the boiler room of a local business. He had dropped out for the spring semester and stayed out of class for the fall semester in order to work on a farm in Nevada long enough to put aside the money for one more session in class.

Then fate intervened.

Snow covered the ground on campus, and the walks were slick as Mike made his way gingerly up the walk to Old Main for his first class of the winter semester. Creeping cautiously up the walk in front of him was a squat and very black boyish looking young man in a long black coat and heavy wool cap. He was struggling to reach the handrail and balance a stack of books at the same time. Then in a flurry, books and papers exploded in space and settled in slow motion into the snow that covered the steps, and this boy who would be a man landed on top of the heap, his black face and overcoat displayed in stark contrast to the soft whiteness of nature's blanket.

The students rushing to beat the bell sidestepped the fallen student and the scattered papers as he struggled to regain his composure.

Mike laid his books on a step next to the ice-laden rail and bent down on one knee. He reached out a hand to the fallen victim of ice and snow and pulled him to a sitting position on the bottom step. Without a word, Mike gathered up the scattered papers and laid them on the books he had stacked in the snow.

"You okay?" Mike asked.

"Okay, mahn. I'm okay, mahn," he said laughing as Mike laid another stack of papers in his outstretched hands.

The pair made their way to class. Then in the crowded halls when class let out, they met again.

"What's your name?" asked the youngish student. A broad grin filled with white teeth reached across the breadth of his black face.

"Mike. What's yours?

"Hugarte."

Mike stumbled to repeat the name, and they both laughed as they parted for the next class.

The semester dragged on for Mike. He saw Hugarte often in the halls and exchanged short greetings between classes. Money was in short supply, and his reserves were fast being depleted. When he returned to his cubicle in the boiler house one evening, he sat on the edge of his bed to read his mail. He hesitated as he stared at a letter from the finance office knowing it was an ultimatum to pay the final payment on his long past due semester's installment or he would have to leave before finals. For several minutes he slapped the envelope across his knee and stared into the lush green of the new springtime leaves bursting into life outside his tiny window.

I just need a couple more weeks, Mike thought, as he stuffed a picture of his mom and dad alongside his clothes he was packing in a box.

He flopped back on the bed and stared out the window into the gathering night. When he finally fell to sleep, the last sliver of the full moon's edge was slipping beneath the window ledge, and the sky was boasting the dawn of a new day. Mike slept hard for several minutes, then sat up abruptly and kicked his feet to the floor. He knew he had to make a deal. He had work waiting on the Nevada ranch. He could earn the money to make the last payment in a couple weeks, but he needed the time. Stuffing the last spoonful of dry cereal into his mouth, he stood up, never taking his eyes off the sunlight sparkling on the dew-laden leaves.

"I'll beg. I'll polish your shoes. I'll lick your boots," Mike practiced almost out loud. He knew then that it was up to him to leave the finance office no option but to let him finish his exams.

Mike burst into the office and leaned on the counter.

"Good morning, Mike." He was well known in this office. "Mrs. Porter will see you in just a minute."

Mike turned toward the wall and examined a large aerial photo of the campus. He couldn't take his eyes off the imposing presence of Old Main that jutted skyward from the center of the campus. It posed as a huge obstacle between him and completion of his third semester at the University of Arkansas.

"Good morning, Mike. Please come in," said Mrs. Porter holding back the door to her office. "Please have a seat."

"I'm here to beg or polish your shoes or lick your boots, but I've got to finish my exams." Mike laid the unopened envelop on Mrs. Porter's desk and pulled up a chair. He sat forward toward Mrs. Porter's desk collecting in his mind the words for the body of his prepared speech and then looked up when Mrs. Porter burst into laughter. She looked across her desk a huge grin ensconced in a thin line of bright red lipstick.

"And," she said, waiting for Mike to continue.

Mike forgot his speech. He slumped back into his chair and folded his hands across his chest.

"I don't know what you can do, ma'am, but I've just got to finish this semester. I'm out of money, my loan installment is being called, and I'm broke. I have a job in Nev—"

"In Nevada," Mrs. Porter cut in. She leaned forward and slid a piece of paper across the desk. Mike picked it up and scanned down the page. It listed all his charges and all his credits and the previous balance. Then at the bottom was noted a final payment leaving a new balance of zero.

Mike looked up. A huge lump grew in his throat, and a weight seemed to press down on his chest.

"Seems there is a God after all," said Mrs. Porter. "A young man came in asking about you yesterday afternoon. He paid your bill in full."

Mike spent the summer cutting and bailing hay in Nevada. When the next semester started, he made the trip by bus back to his cubbyhole in the boiler room. On the bed was a note.

"Call me."

Mike knew the handwriting. He made the call, and that afternoon a car arrived. He moved into the far more than modest surroundings of Hugarte's apartment.

Final exams were looming, and graduation was just a short step away when Hugarte began plying Mike with questions about the process of dating.

"Mike, Mike, I have one date." Hugarte burst into the room and leapt into a recliner by the window. He spun the chair around and bared his teeth in that familiar grin. "That lady in the nurse's office, you know, the one in your class. She say 'yes'!"

"Jessica?" Mike threw his head back and laughed.

"Saturday afternoon."

"Where you going?" asked Mike.

"Don' know. Just dinner." Hugarte got up and walked to the window overlooking a lush garden. "Just dinner," he repeated.

Mike was sleeping when Hugarte slipped into the room and crawled into bed. He stared into the night pushing sleep aside with memories of his first date.

When Mike arrived very early for a review class for his first exam, Jessica was sitting at the table next to where he usually sat. He shoved his books under his chair and sat down.

"I thought he'd never ask," she said reaching over and resting her soft brown hand on Mike's arm. "You know he comes to the nurse's office with any lame excuse. I thought all this time he had his eye on the head nurse. About died when he asked me to dinner. He said to dress up, but when that limousine pulled up, my heart started pounding and my knees turned to jello."

"Limousine?" Mike pulled back and stared. "Where'd he take you for dinner?"

Jessica sat back in her chair and grinned. "I'm too embarrassed to say."

The classroom was beginning to fill when one of Jessica's friends burst into the room and sat on the table in front of Mike. She threw her hands up and flailed the air with her feet and screamed, "San Francisco, we love you, we *love* you!"

Class began, but Mike couldn't concentrate. The vision of a limousine with a small, dark skinned, boyish young man in the back played across his mind blotting out the discussion.

When class let out, he reached out and tugged on the sleeve of Jessica's friend.

"I've got to know," Mike said.

"You didn't hear? They flew to San Francisco! In a private jet! Thought she was lying at first, but signed menus and pictures with the Mr. Mardikian and his staff, a signed copy of his book that's been in the news lately, and limousines don't lie."

Mike was stunned. He stood leaning against the wall for several minutes as crowds of students brushed past. He skipped his next class and returned to his apartment. Hugarte was sitting at his desk studying for an exam. He looked up as Mike entered then took a bite out of an apple and returned to his reading.

"You're not going to say anything?" Mike asked sitting across the desk from his roommate.

"What's to say, mahn?"

"I thought this date was just for dinner."

"'T was." Hugarte didn't look up from his book.

"You don't just fly half way across the country to take a girl on a dinner date. You go to a place close by and have a nice dinner."

Hugarte took another bite out of his apple and placed it on the desk. He leaned forward and stretched his uplifted palms across the desk.

"Where else should I have gone? You just said to take her to dinner." Hugarte was puzzled.

"But San Francisco," Mike choked on the words. "Why San Francisco?"

Hugarte shrugged. He picked up his apple and leaned back looking over his book.

"That's the only restaurant I know," he said turning a page.

To Steal a Trailer 101

Marty pulled the bag of ice away from his eye and looked into the face staring back at him in the mirror. He pushed gently on the puffy flesh, then curled back his lip with his finger and examined the cut along its edge. He pushed the ice gently back against the tender flesh and picked up his fishing pole.

The morning air was tepid and damp on the porch of the stilted cabin that was nestled among a grove of trees at the edge of the bayou. A wooden walk led through the trees to a clearing at the end of a muddy road that led back to town seven miles away.

Marty dropped his hook into the brackish water and watched as a man stepped cautiously across the gaps in the walkway where boards were broken or missing.

To steal correctly, it should be done at night. Any thief understands this as the first rule of a good thief. Yet Marty didn't have to follow this rule because he had a bill of sale on the travel trailer that was "legit." Well, at least it would look that way if he happened to be questioned.

It was on a Sunday afternoon when Marty drove into his brother-in-law's yard. John was relaxing in a hammock in the shade of an oak tree in the back yard. He pulled the last can of beer from the ice chest at his side and handed it to Marty.

"Here's to a deal that's gonna work," John said holding up his beer in a toast, then tipping it to his lips with an exaggerated, boastful display. "I'll be gone for a couple of days, so you can get that trailer anytime after about five this afternoon."

"I got that bill of sale ready," Marty said pulling a piece of paper from his shirt pocket. "Just need you to sign it right here. It'll disappear. Then you can let your insurance man know it was stolen so you can collect the insurance."

"Yeah, that'll work," John said laying his head back and closing his eyes. He pushed the cold beer against his cheek. "Probably take a couple weeks to get my money though."

"Here, sign this. I got a lot to do." Marty laid the paper on a *True Detective* magazine and held out a pen toward John.

It just follows that habits don't die easily so when he knew his brother-in-law was out of town, Marty made his way to the barn and hooked up to the trailer. He eased down the drive and pulled onto the highway at three o'clock in the morning. By noon, Marty had enough money in exchange for the trailer to buy the tractor he had wanted for several years.

It had been three weeks since the deal was made. Marty turned the key in the ignition and listened to the purr of the engine of his new tractor. It was a beauty. Compact, clean, and barely used. He had driven a hard bargain. Cold hard cash always resonates well when it comes to dealing in the hills of the Ozarks. He wheeled the tractor out of the shed and dropped the plow into the dense black soil of his garden behind the house. He was making his last pass when his wife, Bets, stepped onto the back porch and held up the phone.

"For you," she shouted.

"Yeah," Marty said putting the phone to his ear. "No way. Deals been done. Can't go back now."

"What's that all about?" asked his wife.

"Insurance wouldn't pay on that trailer, and John wants some money for it." Marty laughed, handing her the phone.

"Well, Lila says the insurance company has been looking for that trailer for about two years because it was stolen out of Missouri," Bets said snapping the phone shut. "Now they won't pay for a trailer that John stole because it was stolen in the first place? What a surprise."

Marty was laughing out loud as he climbed onto the tractor and eased it back into the shed. He was closing the doors when the front bumper of a pickup appeared at the edge of the gravel lane in front of the house. He walked through the gate and down the drive.

Bob was stepping out of his pickup when Marty came from behind the house. He had a mean look about him, and his fists were doubled up.

"I want my money back," Bob said as he approached.

"What's this all about?" Marty asked, stopping defensively in the drive.

"Ya sold me a durn stolen trailer. Sheriff picked it up this morning. If it wasn't for the bill of sale you gave me, I'd be in jail right now. It seems that whoever you bought it from filed with his insurance on a trailer that has a long history of being stolen. Three times it has been reported stolen by three different people who are all now being accused of stealing it. When I went to license it the title was flagged, and the sheriff came to retrieve it." Bob relaxed a little and twisted his toe in the gravel of the driveway. "I just want my money back, and we'll call everything square."

Marty looked over his shoulder at the closed doors on the shed. He shifted nervously.

"Can't get you money I don't have." Marty squinted into the sun. "Spent it the day I sold the trailer."

"Yeah. Said you were buyin' a tractor." Bob tucked his fists into the bib of his overalls. "I reckon I'll just have to settle for that tractor, won't I?"

"Can't do that," said Marty. "A deal's a deal. Fair and square."

"Warn't fair and warn't square. Ya cheated me with a stolen trailer. I'll be back tomorrow night with a car hauler. I'm gonna get my money or the tractor. You best have one or th'other when I get here."

Bob stared long at Marty and opened the door to his pickup.

"Hey, I want that bill of sale I gave you on the trailer," Marty shouted.

"Too late. Sheriff's got it." Bob slammed the door and drove off.

Marty got home early from work at the feed mill the next afternoon. He was tired and upset as he pulled up in front of his house where a sheriff's deputy was parked in his driveway.

Marty sat looking intently at the unwanted visitor, then got out, and walked cautiously alongside the cruiser.

"Can I help you?" Marty asked when the deputy rolled down his window.

"You Marty Harkins?" the deputy asked.

"Yeah. Whatcha want?"

The deputy pulled a piece of paper from the top of his clipboard then pushed open the door and stepped out.

"I believe that you gave a man by the name of Bob Walstone a bill of sale on a trailer you sold him. An insurance claim for theft was filed by John Billings on that same trailer. Unless you can show some proof of a legal purchase, I'm going to have to place you under arrest for grand larceny." He looked into Marty's eyes, searching for clues about the questionable transactions that he was uncovering. A gray pallor crept up from Marty's collar as the color drained from his face.

"I got a bill a sale. Made a fair deal." Marty walked briskly toward the house with the deputy close behind.

"Bets," he shouted at his wife standing in the door-way. "Get that copy I made of the bill of sale outta the desk drawer."

The deputy took the paper that Marty handed him and read down the page.

"Please come with me for a minute. We need to talk this over," the deputy said walking toward his car. He reached through the open window and took another sheet of paper off the clipboard and compared the signatures.

"It seems that the man who gave you this bill of sale is the same man who filed a claim of theft with his insurance. I have a pretty clear idea about what's going on," the deputy said, "so let's make this easy. I'm going to call for a man to come down and get a tractor that Mr. Walstone says you bought with the money he paid you for the trailer. I'll have it put into a yard until we can sort this thing out. You do have the tractor, don't you?"

"Uh, er, no, not really. Never picked it up," Marty stammered.

"Pretty nice garden back there," the deputy said, stretching to look over the backyard fence. "Heck of a lot of shovelin' on a hot afternoon." He reached through the window of his cruiser and keyed the mic on his radio.

"I'm going to need some backup and a search warrant unless, uh"—he looked at the paper in his hand—"uh, Mr. Harkins here will let me take a look around."

Marty was sitting on the front porch staring at the ground. He stood up and walked to the cruiser.

"Hey, officer, sir," he said haltingly. "I need to call my attorney."

"Just wait right here for a moment," said the deputy spinning Marty around and slapping him in handcuffs. "Yeah, right away," he said to the dispatcher who came over the radio asking about a wrecker. He opened the door of the cruiser and assisted Marty into the back seat.

Marty watched as the driver backed his "roll-off" wrecker up the driveway. The handcuffs dug into his skin as he tried to make himself more comfortable in the backseat of the patrol car. The neighbors down the lane were watching from the front of their house, and his wife had planted her feet firmly on the top step of the porch. Her apron hung limply over her ample bosom, and the bright silver of a stirring spoon flashed in the sun as she flipped it up and down in her clenched fist.

The deputy led Marty down a long hall leading from the back of the jail. He was staring at the floor as they entered the booking room.

"Sit right over there," the deputy said, pointing to a bench along the wall.

Marty looked up and stared into the face of John who was slumped against the wall. He sat down, and without a word he leaned forward to ease the pressure of the cuffs holding his hands behind his back.

"Wife's calling a bondsman," he began trying to exude an aura of confidence. "They got no evidence. My attorney'll chew 'em up. We'll own this jail when he gets done with these amateurs." Marty brushed back a strand of long hair from his cheek with his shoulder. "Should be outta here in half an hour."

Two weeks had passed when Marty climbed into the passenger's seat beside his wife.

"Had to sell the rent house and your pickup to get you out of jail," she began. "The attorney needs another five grand just to keep you out. The prosecutor wants you arrested again before you get home for forging those documents, and Bob has come by at least five times wanting his money back. You screwed up big time, Marty. You never were too bright, but this one beats all."

Marty slumped down in the seat peering over the edge of the door as the fence posts along the lane leading to his house flew by.

"I'm not putting up with your crap any more. I want out of this marriage. Talked to an attorney about a divorce last week. You screwed up for the last time." Bets turned the car into the driveway. "He says the house and land are mine because I inherited them from my folks. You can have the old pickup out behind the barn and your tools. I keep the car. I got your stuff packed up. Your sister in Louisiana says you can stay in that cabin on the bayou for a few days,, but I want you out of here today. You better check with the judge before you leave the state for your sis's cabin. I know you can't leave here till after the hearing. Mr. Henderson at the feed mill says he's had enough of your crap and doesn't want you coming back. Your future around here looks pretty bleak."

Marty followed Bets across the porch and reached for the door. Bets threw her body sideways, pushing him out of the way. Marty grabbed for the door as she let it slam behind her.

"Here," Bets said flipping some papers across the table as Marty followed her into the kitchen. "Sign them at all the red tabs. It'll make all this a whole lot easier."

"I'll get an attorney. You'll end up with nuthin'," Marty growled.

"Stealing a stolen trailer isn't going to make you look too smart when presented to the judge. Going to make it kinda hard for him to see your point of view. Check with John. Lila bailed him out just to have him arrested again the next day. Seems they found he had stolen more than just that trailer."

Marty stared at the papers on the table then walked to the front door. He pushed open the screen door and walked right into a right hook that Bob landed on his left eye.

Marty staggered for a moment and then caught his balance. Bob was retreating down the steps when Marty cleared his vision.

"Might be the only satisfaction I'll get, but I intend to get my money back if I have to take it out of your hide a piece at a time." Bob slammed the door on his pickup and spun his tires as he sped away, spewing dust and gravel high into the air.

Marty slapped a mosquito on his neck with his free hand and glanced at the tip of his pole that jerked lightly at the tug of a fish nibbling at his bait. He shifted nervously as the stranger grasped the rickety wooden handrail that led to his front porch.

"You Marty Harkins?"

"Might be, who's askin'?"

The man pulled a photo from his shirt pocket.

"I'm takin' you back to Fayetteville. Seems you missed your appointment with the judge. You know, the date about that stolen trailer." The man stepped quickly up onto the porch blocking Marty's escape back into the cabin. He grabbed Marty and slammed him against the wall and wrenched his hands down and back, slapping handcuffs on him in one motion.

"Took a year to find ya, so let's not do it like this," the man said. "That rotten old house of yours just paid the bail, but it didn't cover the bond. I don't plan to cover that bond myself, so I'm going to deliver you to the judge instead."

"Watch the eye," Marty squealed.

"Took a long time for that shiner Bob Walstone gave you to heal. Been almost a year," the man chuckled as he led Marty to a car parked at the end of the wooden walkway.

"Naw, the chick I been livin' with done this last night," said Marty shifting his weight away from the pressure of his hands jammed against the back seat. "Just hope this shack'll still be standin' if I survive what Bets is gonna do when I get to Fayetteville." He leaned his head back and closed his eyes.

The Smallest Loaf

To Isaac she was gorgeous in the slightly tattered trappings of her red dress. Isaac sat on the floor with his elbow resting lightly on the back of the ottoman on which she sat staring at the familiar blank spot on the wall. He knew she was listening to each word as he talked. In the two years since he carried her to the orphanage from where he found her curled up under a hedge she had not spoken a word. Today had been special because she had twisted up the corners of her mouth in a shy smile as she took her place on the well-worn ottoman.

Orphanages were a harsh place for children during the depression in the Midwest cities. They were a refuge, of course, from the gutters and back alleys where dangers lurked, but there was little money. Those who were in charge were pressed by the grueling facts that each day was another struggle to find enough flour and meat to feed the growing children they had scooped from the risks of living on the street. At times the pressures of squabbling hordes of children and the constant struggle to keep the doors open pushed the managers to extremes in the daily regimen that to some seemed cruel. For Isaac these extremes were a shield in this Spartan haven in which he could languish from the abuses of the bigger children who tormented him when he was living alone in a cardboard shelter behind that hedge.

Every evening, Isaac struggled to reach the counter where Mr. Bitkin would supervise as the children pushed and shoved their way in a long line. Each would take a loaf of bread, then find a place at a table where a bowl of gruel would complete the fare, which ended the day.

Isaac had long since expected no more than the smallest loaf to be waiting when he reached the counter. He was the smallest boy at the orphanage, and the bigger boys and girls did their best to push him to the end of the line. But he was clever.

When the line began to form, Isaac would wait for the opportunity to duck beneath the front of the counter and reach up over the side to snatch a loaf of bread before all the larger loaves were gone. He had learned every expression and every signal on the face of Mr. Bitkin and had developed a routine that would keep him from the feigned harsh glare and discipline of the older boys that kept order in the daily regimen of the evening meal.

With his prize in hand, Isaac would hustle across the room and place the nice loaf on the table in front of his friend who was waiting. She would bite her lip, thrust her hands into her lap and turn her face away from him covering it with her shoulder.

Each day, Isaac spent time talking to her, but she always sat staring at the wall, her dark curls draping across her face like a curtain to keep the world out. But at the end of each day, the delivery gave him a sense of relief.

Moving to the end of the line he would wait knowing that the smallest loaf would remain alone on the tray when his turn came to approach the counter and he'd dutifully say, "Thank you, Mr. Bitkin." When he took his place across from his friend a bowl of thin soup with tiny specks of meat would be waiting. He would break a piece of bread from the end of the tiny loaf and dip it into the soup and slowly put it into his mouth prolonging the pleasure of this evening ritual.

Today had started the same as every other day. He had spent time talking with his friend who sat facing the wall. The ritual had been the same. He had sneaked a nice loaf for his friend, then took his place at the end of the line and waited to take the tiny loaf that would remain. He smiled as he broke off a small piece of his own smaller than usual loaf. A shiny spot in the center of his loaf glistened in the dim light. He picked bits of bread away from the gleaming speck with his frail fingers then cautiously dipped the pieces in his soup and placed them on his tongue, not daring to take his eyes off the foreign matter nestled in the center of the broken loaf resting in his hand. With trembling fingers Isaac pulled on the glistening object and slid a brand new silver dollar into his hand and the tears began to roll down his cheeks. He stared at the prize and clutched it to his chest. Looking through his tears, he saw Mr. Bitkin standing behind the counter looking through glazed eyes over his glasses. A huge grin spread slowly across his face. He winked, squeezing a flood of tears down his face. He knew that each day the smallest loaf went to the biggest heart, and from the smallest sacrifices came the greatest rewards.

Isaac dodged the horse-drawn milk wagon and gave the driver a cheery wave, then cut down an alley and across the river bridge. He stood for several minutes staring at the red dress in the window of the familiar used clothing store. The mental vision of his friend walking shyly into the room in her new red dress gave him the courage to push open the door and walk to the counter. He reached into his pocket and pulled out the coin. For several seconds he stared at the beauty of the unexpected gift and laid it on the counter.

"That one," he said to the lady leaning across the counter toward him. He pointed toward the window with a grin.

Gas, Fire, and Suicide

She was depressed. No, the doctors had not diagnosed this, but Angela was done. Her husband was away on the road, and Roberta, his "secretary," kept calling the house to see if he had gotten home and left messages to be sure he called the minute he got in.

Secretary? Yeah, right. If that was true, she would know how to contact him wherever he was because he checked in with the dispatcher every day.

Angela had decided when he climbed into the cab of his truck and pulled onto the highway that this was the time for her to check out. He would be home in a few days and would find her body here in the kitchen where she had decided to gas herself. She had turned the gas on full blast, sat back in the corner on the floor, and waited. Sweat was pouring down her face. She took a towel and wiped the sweat from between her

breasts, then leaned forward and shoved her face into
the towel.

How long should this take? she wondered, staring at
her feet from beneath the towel.

This had not been a fly-by-night plan. She had prepared for weeks to make this go just right. The kitchen
windows were closed tight, and the doors had been
sealed with duct tape. She even had a pillow on the floor
in the corner where she sat. *Might as well be comfortable when you check out,* she had philosophized. When
her old man would find her, he could take a good look.
Then he'd know what a beauty he had really lost.

The phone rang. Angela sat waiting for the answering machine to pick up. She listened, then jumped to
her feet and grabbed the receiver when she realized it
was her younger brother.

"Hello?" she gasped, brushing the hair back with
the towel.

"You okay?" he asked. "Sounds like you've been
running. Hey, 'Gela, I got some papers I need you to
sign. Got to get Dad's estate finished up."

"Uh, can't we do this tomorrow?" Angela asked,
looking furtively around the room. She had not really
given this turn of events any thought. She was Bobby's
pet. He did everything to make her happy. When Milt
was on the road, he'd come by every couple of days just
to see that she was okay. Until now, nothing else had
mattered except the feeling of victory she felt when she
thought of the horror that Milt would experience when
he came home to find her lifeless form propped up in

the corner of the kitchen. But now another dynamic was being introduced. The prospect that Bobby might be the one to find her lifeless body terrified her.

"I'm just down the street. On my way to check on a job about a mile from your house, so I figured I'd come by and get this done. Be there in about two minutes." He hung up the phone before Angela could object.

Angela quickly twisted the knobs on the stove, turning off the gas and shoved the door to the garage wide open. When Bobby rang the bell, she was ripping off the last strip of duct tape from around the door. She looked in the mirror by the entry door and was aghast at the always perfectly made up face staring back at her. Her dark hair was drenched, and her blouse was soaked in sweat. Black streaks of mascara ran in rivulets down her cheeks. But worst of all, her beautiful skin looked like a tomato with white blotches scattered over the surface.

Bobby jumped back in mock surprise when he looked at the bedraggled vision of his beautiful sister standing as if she had just finished her third marathon.

"Been hard at it?" Bobby said stepping through the door.

Angela motioned to a chair without responding.

Bobby walked across the room and started to sit down but jumped back when a blast of hot air from the kitchen slammed into his face. He stepped through the door and stared at the taped up air-conditioning vent on the ceiling. For a moment he stood motionless staring.

Angela's heart was jumping in her chest as she realized that she had not done a complete job of cleaning up the evidence of her macabre plan.

"Come here," Bobby motioned.

Angela walked cautiously across the room realizing that the person she most adored could have been the person she hurt the most. In her anger, she had not figured him into the formula. Since Dad had died, she and Bobby had been left alone. The loneliness had been pressing down on her for weeks. Added to this was stress of a wandering husband. The combined load was more than she could bear. All reason and consideration for the only other person left of their family for whom she really cared had been buried in her mad dash to punish her wayward husband. Sanity had been trashed, and she had become obsessed with the idea that Milt be overwhelmed with guilt for spurning his fealty to their marriage vows.

Bobby took Angela by the shoulders and gently backed her up to a chair by the kitchen table. He closed the door and without a word began taping the edges with the roll of tape he found on the counter.

"What are you doing?" Angela asked quietly.

Bobby didn't answer. He peeled a strip of tape from the roll and ran it along the floor sealing off the gap above the tile, then twisted the knobs on the stove and watched as each burner came alive with a bright blue flame. "If you're going to check out, you're not going without me."

Bobby pulled a chair from the table and leaned back against the wall. He put his hands behind his head and closed his eyes.

"I figure three, maybe four hours with the stove turned up high we'll have worked up a real sweat." Bobby didn't move. "Give us a while to think. Maybe we can talk about what a grand life we've had. You know, it's been a good run. Twenty-three years knowing one of the neatest people in the world. There couldn't be a better time to go. We're right on top of the crest. We haven't had to worry about much. You have a husband who loves and cares about you. A brother who adores the most beautiful sister he has even though you are my only sis."

Angela stared at her brother in disbelief. She wanted to get up and turn off the stove, but she couldn't move. Bobby just sat with his eyes closed waiting.

"You going to get that?" Bobby asked when the phone rang. He didn't move.

"This is Roberta," a voice said when the answering machine picked up. "Please call me and let me know when you expect Milt to get in. I have some papers I need the two of you to sign the minute he arrives."

Bobby began to smile and then leaned forward, bringing the front legs of his chair to the floor with a thud. He ceremoniously twisted the knob on each burner slowly, watching the flame dwindle then go out. He stood for a moment looking at the darkened burners then sat down in the chair and leaned back.

"Yep, without a doubt the most beautiful sister I've got. Not too bright sometimes, but beautiful." Bobby began to laugh. "Losing Dad was tough, but losing you would be more than I could take."

Angela got up and yanked open the kitchen door ripping loose the tape from the frame.

"How was I supposed to know? I've never killed myself before."

Bobby drew his sister to him pulling her tight to his chest. He nuzzled her dampened hair and brushed his cheek across hers.

"It's time you snapped out of this downhill slide. I can't make it without you, and I have too much left to do to check into the netherworld right now. Milt sold his truck, you know, just so he could spend more time with you. He'll be working with me starting tomorrow."

"Is this for real?" Angela twisted around in Bobby's arms and leaned back staring into his face.

"You bet it's for real. Tomorrow you pick out the furniture for your new house. It'll be ready for you to move in this week. Remind me to call and have that gas stove pulled out though. They say electric is the way to go anyway.

"And don't forget to call Roberta. She needs you two to go by the bank and sign the loan the minute Milt gets in. You know real estate agents. Have to have all the t's crossed and i's dotted.

"Now let's get this kitchen cleaned up and be sure you pull that tape off the register on the ceiling! And by the way, sis, you don't know about the new house. Know what I mean? And the next time you want to check out, blow out the pilot lights before you turn on the burners!"

Barmaid in High Heels

She was big, she was beautiful, and she was stunning in her trademark red high heels. She moved behind the bar with the smoothness of a phantom whose form was transparent but solid in its commanding presence as she slid drink after drink along the bar to her adoring patrons. The rustle of her miniskirt each time she stooped to pull a new bottle from the cooler behind the bar drew glances from her audience who ogled through blurred eyes for a glimpse of skin or a bit of cleavage from under the low-cut line of her blouse.

Flo was the queen of the riverfront. She said little, but her subtle smile lit a spark in every patron that hoped that tonight might be the night that this diva serving drinks would choose to leave with him. But each night she would graciously and tenderly make the last call then gently but firmly usher her admirers out the door or guide those unfit to drive toward a called-up waiting cab.

Every patron that came to the bar night after night went away knowing that he would be in Flo's dreams when she lay down to catch a few hours sleep before she went to her second mysterious job in the morning. But each night the last call would be made and the bar would be empty as she stacked the chairs on the tables and swept the floor. Then as quietly as she moved behind the bar, she would pull the door shut behind her, slide the key into the lock, and step into her waiting cab.

On a hot, sultry night, a stranger sat near the painted window along the abandoned sidewalk. He was coddling a tall mug of draft beer between his crusty hands and stared at the head of foam as if counting the bubbles as they burst. As if performing the prescribed procedures of a ritual, the stranger would lift his mug to his lips leaving a narrow line of foam on his dark mustache. With each sip of beer, he would quietly set his mug back on the table and continue counting bubbles. When the last speck of foam had slid down the side of the glass leaving a golden disk at the bottom of the mug, he would look up and without words call for a refill with his black eyes glistening from under the wide brim of his Stetson.

Flo slid the empty mug across the table and set it on her tray. She replaced it with a mug brimming over with a head of beer that spilled down the side of the chilled glass leaving a wet circle on the dry paper of a fresh napkin. The stranger didn't look up as he peeled three one-dollar bills from the top of a stack in the center of the table and slid them toward Flo. He lifted his massive hand just enough to let her know that the change was for her, then resumed coddling his fresh mug and counting the bursting bubbles.

It was late when Flo made her last call. She was working feverishly behind the bar getting the drinks ready so she could deliver them to the tables before the clock on the wall struck two. Spinning around, she set four frozen mugs on the counter and stared into the barrel of an automatic pistol resting lightly in the steady hand of the towering stranger she had just served.

The stranger flicked the end of the barrel just slightly toward the cash register. With his left hand, he slid a canvas bag across the counter. Two stunned patrons sat at a table by the wall, and a man leaned against the padded rail at the end of the bar, his bottle of beer suspended just above the smooth wood of the rosewood top.

The stranger looked back at Flo and flicked the pistol again.

"In the bag," he said quietly, pointing his pistol toward the register. Flo stared at the barrel of the pistol pointed at her chest. It looked as big as a cannon; then its giant size began to dwindle on a rising tide of anger in her mind. She started to move toward the register then without warning she heaved four mugs in the face of the stranger. As he staggered back, she caught the toe of her high heel shoe on the edge of the ice machine's hopper. Shoving hard, she pushed her body forward and up, clearing the rail of the service deck and hitting the stranger full in his startled face as he retreated backwards from the onslaught of four mugs pummeling him simultaneously in the forehead, face, and chest.

The force of Flo's frame and the weight of her ample bosom drove the stranger back as she grappled for anything of substance to hang on to as the two hit the floor with a thud. The momentum and the force of gravity pulling the flying barmaid down on top of the stranger sent the pistol skittering across the floor as his head met the resistance of the hardwood. The sound of two bodies slamming down lingered as the stunned patrons watched the drama unfold.

Flo lay still for a moment, the abundance of her thighs straddling the slender waist of the stranger pinned to the floor. She breathed in heavily waiting for the next move from the man beneath her whose face was buried in her bosom.

There was a snicker from across the room, then laughter. Flo struggled to push herself up onto her hands and gazed into the terrified eyes of her assailant. He didn't move but stared, gasping desperately for air.

A feeling of compassion welled up from within Flo. It was a feeling she couldn't explain. A feeling that shouldn't be there but one she couldn't control. Sadness rushed into the back of her mind but was overpowered by the anger that drove her over the bar and into the face of her assailant. Rolling onto her side, she leaned on her elbow and watched the supine form of the man who moments ago seemed a giant but had morphed into the form of a boy. Pushing herself to her feet, she pulled out a chair and sat watching and wondering how a quiet evening had suddenly turned violent and reverted as suddenly to a crushed silence shattered only by the cacophony of coughing and gasping of this man who had moments ago been the epitome of strength and control.

A stream of exploding light burst into the room as two police officers stepped in and planted themselves on the hardwood floor with their hands on their pistols. They stared at the man sitting on the floor surrounded by three grinning men and a woman sitting in a chair.

"This the joker who tried to rob you, Miss Flo?" the first officer asked as he entered.

Flo nodded. She patted a hand resting on her shoulder, the gentle hand of the patron who spent each evening sitting at the end of the bar. The officers pushed the assailant to the floor, cuffed him, then lifted him to his feet. Flo looked up into the subdued eyes of a giant of a man who moments ago seemed so small. He towered above her as he stood with his hands behind him locked in the grasp of the cuffs snapped around his wrists.

"I thought I was going to die," he said staring at Flo's bosom bursting from her blouse with each breath. "I thought I was going to suffocate in a mountain of boobs," he said looking over his shoulders as the officers ushered him out the door.

And He Laughed

There was rarely a serious moment when you were with George. It wasn't just his jesting or cutting up, but it was his sense that everything had a humorous aspect that should be exploited. He could see a reason to laugh or poke fun in the way a tree was silhouetted against the fading sunset or the comic look on the face of a bird sitting on a wire.

George was deeply religious, but even in his approach to God there was humor. He read the stories in the Bible and found the light side of the way people lived or how the twists of fate on individuals in ancient times differed little from the twists and turns that we experience today. To him, life was just plain fun.

To describe George as clumsy would be a far away attempt at summing him up in a word. But he even found canisters of laughter in his own comparisons with his sister who was a professional ballet dancer. He loved to sing in church but found humor is his own discordant attempts when put up against the beauty and flare of his other sister who toured the world singing opera.

George's parents were distraught that their son was not able to conform to the regimen of their desire to thrust him into the world of genteel grace of his sisters. He graced them instead with raucous stories of their attempts to impute in him a bit of culture and beauty.

When just a young boy, he was plunged into the boots of a pair of ice skates. His sisters had become accomplished figure skaters, so "Why not George?" his parents reasoned. It was not for lack of effort that he described himself as the mop that kept the ice clean. His focus was more on the hilarious view looking up from his fallen pose at his friends twirling about on the ice than his desire to transform his ungainly body into a thing of beauty.

His teachers were constantly stressed to see him arrive with shining blades and all the accoutrements of an accomplished figure skater but failing miserably to advance his skills to the next level. But the money was always there, and his parents were determined. In desperation, he was moved from the drills of cutting figures on the ice to the rigors of speed.

Finally George was thrust into an element where he could excel. He was the fastest and most daring of all his competitors on the ice. He honed his skills at getting off the line at the snap of the gun. He perfected his technique with his skates until it became letter perfect. There was no one among his peers that could match his start and the dash to the first turn, but he never won a race. Hours of practice and a myriad falls during his practices got him no closer to accomplishing the art of making the turns. He crashed, he fell, he slowed, he sped up, and he laughed and joked. But nothing propelled him closer to that cherished first to the finish.

It was his spectacular crashes that were fodder for innuendoes and imagery of the circumstances in life. A wall being raised on a new house was pushed too far and came crashing to the ground in pieces. To George it was a wonderful event that sounded like the crash on the second turn in the race at the regional trials. A new comer on the job would come under his raucous scrutiny because his clumsy moves "looked like me when I was trying a triple lutz." A truck driver backing onto a location would be told he was so lousy that he should take figure skating lessons from him "'cause if you're going to crash and tear things up, I can at least show you how to make it spectacular."

To George, there was nothing sacred, and there was nothing that wasn't funny.

Out of high school, he went to work but couldn't keep a job. He swept the city working at every type of work. He served in a fancy restaurant with tables draped in white linen until the owner, a friend of his father's, gave up and risked the ire of his friend and fired him.

"Well," the owner explained, "it's one thing to slide a steak off into the mayor's lap, but when he doubled up with laughter and pointed to the ridiculous look on the mayor's face as he scraped the mess from his tuxedo, it was just more than I could take."

That was George's legacy as he bounced from job to job. He had an uncanny knack for laughing at the wrong time. He laughed at the owner's wife when she missed the driveway by an inch and parked on the lawn of her new house on which he was working and thus was sent looking for another job. He laughed at the boss when he ducked under a brace on a wall and put a gash in his head demanding three stitches and again was sent packing. He laughed when he arrived on a job and joined the crew peering into a small lake that had formed where a basement had been dug and formed up for the foundations of a house. "Looks like you should have designed this with an engine and propeller," he said laughing at the architect. "I kept telling you this heap looks more like a ship than a house."

"Get out!" yelled the architect. "I can't take your insolence any more. I'll see to it you never work in this town again."

George was laughing and yelling insults at the architect who stood at the edge of the chasm shaking his head. He got into his pickup and drove off laughing and waving on his way to his next job. He never had trouble getting a job. It was just keeping them that gave him trouble. He went to his parents for help. They sent him to a psychologist to search for a key that would lock the door so that his humor could only to be opened at the appropriate time, but the key never fit. He continued to waltz through his young adult years in the work force seeing the humor in any situation no matter how serious.

Several sessions with the psychologist and several jobs came and went when George had the opportunity to interview for a job at the local navy base. He charmed his way through the interview with laughter and smart remarks. He captivated the interest of the personnel director with his wit and intelligence and was asked to show up for orientation on a construction crew the next day.

There was never a question about George's ability, his honesty, or his work ethics, but he continued to draw the ire of his superiors with his jocularity and macabre humor of every aspect of what he or the crew or the big bosses were doing. He could find a joke in the design of a tangled mass of some bent up re-bar or the way the backhoe operator was digging a ditch. Nothing was off limits to his jibes and ridicule.

The foreman was excited one morning when a truck laden with tracks of a huge dozer arrived at the base. He waved his arms and guided the driver into an open space beside a crane. He worked with a flare for a compliment of 'white hats' that stood by watching, sweltering in the confines of their suits and ties.

George stood at a distance watching and joking as the tracks were lifted and set on the ground. A second truck pulled into the space carrying the dozer. The boss examined the gigantic piece of equipment with an expert eye. He paced about, directing the riggers and demanding that every cable was attached without a twist or kink. The lines were drawn tight, and the boss rechecked the connections. He was perturbed when George slipped in alongside and nudged him with his elbow.

"Sir," George said in a rare serious tone. "That cable is attached to the wrong lifting eye. The one you're using is just to remove the hood. It's not strong— "

"Oh, shut up, and get out of the way," shouted the boss, crazed by the interruption of this lowly laborer.

"But sir, it's just welded to sheet metal and—" George tried to explain.

"Get out. You're always making trouble," shouted the foreman cutting him off.

He signaled the operator to start lifting the dozer above the rails of the lowboy so the truck could be driven clear of the load. Very slowly the giant moved up. The foreman walked about watching the progress with his expert eye. His body language exuded the confidence of a man above the subservient lowlifes who stood about ready to jump at his every command. His moves were staged to impress the 'white hats' that he was totally in control. A closed fist signaled the operator to stop the lift. The foreman walked around the rear of the lowboy checking the height to make sure the load would clear as the truck pulled clear.

There was a light snap. George stepped away from the watching crowd of workers and stared at the lifting eye.

Another snap cut the silenced air as the men stood watching to see what kind of a prank George might have contrived.

"It's going to cut loose!" George shouted. "Get away!" He bolted toward the staring 'white hats' waving his arms as the eye broke loose with the crack of a cannon. The cable twisted skyward in a slow motion tangle as the load shifted tearing apart the strands of an adjacent cable. The dozer swung around like a tormented animal facing its attacker. A corner dropped. A third cable ripped and tore, singing as it split the air in its race into space. The dozer rolled dragging the boom of the crane with it as it hit the rail of the lowboy driving the massive steel frame into the earth. It heaved slightly and then lay motionless across the twisted rails as the broken boom of the crane sagged and fell with a roar across it as though laying claim to a captured trophy. Even the breeze was still as the stunned crowd stood not daring to move in a rising cloud of dust.

Then George began to snicker. He tried to remain calm and serious, but the humor he saw transcended the impulse. He doubled over with laughter. He fell to the dirt and kicked his feet into the air and guffawed before the gawking crowd.

"George, you're fired! I want you out of here right now," screamed the foreman pointing his finger toward the front gate. "Get out! Get out now!"

George was still laughing when he got to his feet and brushed the dust from his pants. He ran his hand through his dark curly hair and stood facing the foreman still laughing without reserve.

"Wait." A 'white hat' walked up and put his hand on George's shoulder.

George's laughter slipped to a chuckle then to a grin.

"Did I hear you correctly? Are you firing this man?" the 'white hat' said, looking intently into the eyes of the foreman.

"Well. Uh, yes. This is a dangerous situation, and he has no business laughing under the circumstances." The foreman looked down and kicked up a small divot in a soft clump of grass at his feet.

"Good. Young man, the machine shop can use a little light humor. They're a bunch of old fuddy duddies that need someone to lighten up the dark corners of that shop. Go see the lead man over there and tell him I sent you. And you, sir," the 'white hat' said turning to the foreman, "be in my office in ten minutes. We have some things in your future to discuss."

An Angel Sent

Dylan lifted the phone from the cradle and jammed it under his jaw.

"Yeah! This is Dylan."

Jim Garber's voice rattled the earpiece pressed against Dylan's ear.

"Got a bad dude just comin' off the cell block. Parole board thinks with a chance he might just become something other than a lifer. Don't know what they're thinkin' sometimes but gotta play the game. Possible you can take a minute and see what you think?"

"Sure. Bring him by," said Dylan. "I need a couple more guys on the line. Gotten thirty-six guys from you in the past couple years. Some good, some bad, but you always steered me straight up."

Jim Garber stepped into Dylan's office without knocking.

"Meet Haydn, Haydn Williams." He motioned to a tall black man whose dark silhouette framed in brilliant sunlight filled the doorway behind him.

"Have a seat, Garber." Dylan motioned to a massive red leather love seat against the wall across from his desk. He pulled his own chair from behind his desk and sank heavily into its plush black leather.

"Sit." Dylan motioned Haydn to a matching red leather armchair behind a marble coffee table.

"You don't look like you have much interest in conforming to the demands of society," Dylan began without further introduction. "Been looking over your record. Nine years in and out of juvenile detention before you were seventeen. Four burglaries; two criminal assaults; two charges of rape, which were dropped; and several drug trafficking charges. Then there was the suspected murder of one of your teachers that the cops couldn't make stick. You finally got caught stealing a box of bullets and got sent up for eleven months for violating probation. That's not the end. You were out of jail for less than two months when you made the brilliant decision to join a buddy and knock off a liquor store. With a gun you and your buddy killed an innocent man who had always tried to help you. Zap! Twenty-five to life."

Dylan paused and swirled an ice cube around in a tall glass of water as he flipped through the stack of papers that made up Haydn's rap sheet. He pushed a button on the intercom without taking his eye off the papers and asked the secretary to bring a couple Pepsis to his guests.

He folded the papers and tossed them to the middle of his desk. Leaning back in his chair, he crossed his legs and looked into the bilious eyes of the man sitting rigidly on the edge of the red leather chair.

"And you want me to get you back on the streets by giving you a job?" Dylan stared into the clouded eyes waiting for a reaction. Slowly Haydn's head lowered under the intense gaze.

"You're a loser, Haydn," Dylan continued. "I can see no pattern of behavior that would give me the confidence to know that you won't steal from me at your first opportunity."

For several seconds Haydn looked down at the gnarled hands folded in his lap, then lifted his head and straightened his back. He was an imposing figure. He had all the equipment to take the bet and win in the game of life but had chosen to take his chances on the "easy way out." Now he was placing a marker on Dylan's table and challenging him to take the bet.

"Sir," he began slowly, "since I was seven I've spent my life breakin' the law. I done lottsa bad things. I've hurt lottsa good people. What you see in my rap sheet shows you that, but what you can't see is the terrible pain right here for some of things I done"—he jabbed his thumb hard into his chest—"I spent seventeen years dying inside for the harm I done to Mr. Jawarski's family."

Tears were running down Haydn's face. He clutched his chest with his giant hand and sobbed.

"Do you know what it is like never to hear from your sisters or even your mama, who won't even come to visit or write? Can you imagine for a moment what it is like to sit in your darkened cell and stare at the tiny bulb hangin' from a wire on the ceiling and cry for just some word about whether your baby sister be graduatin' from high school or your older sister's baby done survived his surgery? Can you imagine what it is like when the warden has to bring you the news that your father is dead and you can't go to the funeral?

"Yeah, you be right to think of me as a loser, but I have spent seventeen years doing my best to make up for my past. I write to my mother every week, but she never answers. Do you know what that does to a man?" Haydn wiped his eyes on his sleeve. "Sir, I come here today to beg you for a chance. I can promise you right now, today, that on my watch you ain't never gonna lose a grain of sand 'cause I know that I'm going to be accused. I ain't got no more chances, sir. This is it."

It was on a Friday that Dylan handed Haydn his paycheck. For the past two years, Haydn had been true to his word. He was never late. He never dragged time on his breaks or at the end of the day. He gave a full day every day and without asking for anything in return but fair pay for a day's work.

"Can I talk with you for a minute?" Haydn asked.

Dylan led him to his office and motioned him to a chair.

Haydn shoved his hand into his pants pocket and pulled out a tattered letter and handed it to Dylan.

"I didn't know who to ask, but will you read this to me?"

Dylan stared at the letter then into Haydn's black face.

"Sir"—he hesitated—"I've had this for a month. You see, I don't know what it says because I can't read."

"But I thought you wrote to your mother every week while in prison," he said, reading the unfamiliar return address on the envelope. "This isn't from your mother," Dylan said, snapping the letter with his finger. "A girlfriend?" he asked with a grin.

"No, a girl I've never met. My mother never writes. Doesn't know I'm even out of prison I suspect because I can't read or write. My friend in prison did all the writing for me. Since I've been out, I haven't written home."

Dylan slipped the point of a letter opener under the flap of the envelope and pulled gently, then slid the paper out. The page was filled in a beautiful hand that expressed the care and feeling of the girl who wrote.

"Dear sir," the letter began:

> I have asked Mr. Beckett at the bank many times for your name and a way to get in touch

with you. He has always said to leave a message with him, and he would see that you get it.

I don't know much about you, but you must be the most wonderful man in the world. I don't know why you have chosen to help me, but since my father died during a robbery at his liquor store when I was just six, I have known there was not enough money for me to go to college. When I graduated from high school, I didn't have the grades I needed for a scholarship because I have had to spend every afternoon working to help my mother keep the store open to feed and clothe my two brothers and twin sisters. But then Mr. Beckett told me there was a savings account that had enough to get me through the first year of college. And the checks began to come, and they have never stopped.

Because of the money you have sent and with the help of my counselors, I will be graduating this spring. I have a job waiting for me in a medical clinic that will give me enough money to go on to medical school. Bobby entered as a freshman this year. He has a full scholarship. Marvin is finishing high school this semester, and the twins are on the honor roll every year.

Mr. Beckett says you don't ever want to be repaid for what you have done, but I can tell you that others will be helped through the years because of the kindness you have sent our way, a kindness that we have begun to repay by being the best citizens we are able.

Haydn sat with his head down and his hands folded in his lap. Dylan squeezed a tear that threatened to roll down his cheek from the corner of his eye and continued:

> Sir, I have received a check each week for four years now. Each week I have put one fourth of that money back into the savings account you started for me nineteen years ago. That money will be used to put my brothers and sisters through college, but more than that, the bank has challenged their employees to help build that account, which now holds thousands of dollars. It is enough to help many struggling students that didn't have a chance like myself.
>
> I am writing you as I have done each month for the past four years hoping that someday you will accept my thanks, which I feel very inadequate to express. When I hand Mr. Beckett this letter as I have done each month, I will ask him again if he can arrange for us to meet. I already know the answer. But this time, along with this letter, I'm handing him a request to change the name of this account from my name to "From an Angel Sent Scholarship Fund."
>
> Gail
>
> P.S. To you, sir, I can only say that angels come in many wrappers, and yours must be lily white!

Haydn lifted his huge black hands and brushed them across his braided hair. He looked up at Dylan and stood up.

"I couldn't read her letters," he said.

"Every month?" Dylan asked.

"Uh huh. Have 'em all stuffed here in my lunch box. Couldn't trust nobody to read 'em. I don't want no honor. I can't earn enough in my lifetime to pay for what I did. The little bit that I can do is not payment. It's a privilege to share the little I have with people more deserving than me. People like my parole officer and Mr. Beckett and you have made me see the goodness in this world."

Haydn laid his hand on the door handle and looked back for just a moment.

"See you Monday morning, sir," he said, leaving Dylan to reflect on the greatness of this simple man.

When he had left, Dylan went to the file and pulled a cancelled check from the folder and noted the name of the bank where it had been deposited into the account of Jawarski Trust.

Dylan was at the bank when the door was unlocked Monday morning. He reached across the desk to Mr. Beckett and handed him a company check.

"Do you know who this man really is?" Dylan asked.

"You bet," he answered. "He's an angel who got his wings after being tempered in the fires of hell." He looked at the check. "You know. This is a nice addition to the fund that Haydn started nineteen years ago. Our bank employees contribute every month a portion of their paychecks to this fund. Haydn waits each week on the sidewalk until the guard is about to lock the door. He will stay here just long enough to hand me his paycheck from your company and to take twenty dollars for his week's spending money. I pay his rent in a little sleazy hotel and the rest goes into this fund."

When Dylan got to his car, he pulled a piece of paper from his pocket and examined the address. It was a place where life on the streets meant little. The yard of the tenement house where he stopped was scattered with junk and broken cars. A group of young men stood guarding the entrance as he approached.

"Looking for Mrs. Mathias," he said to a boyish man who seemed to be the leader.

He examined Dylan warily for a moment; then he pointed to the stairs.

"Third floor, third door on the left. Been sick, so bang on the door." He gestured to make sure Dylan knew what to do.

In a darkened hall, Dylan waited for a response to his knock. A male voice growled from behind the scarred door.

"Who you?"

"I'm looking for Mrs. Clarissa Mathias," Dylan said, mustering up a note of confidence.

"Ain't nobody here of that name."

"Who is it?" a quiet female voice asked.

"Don' know. Some guy lookin' fer ya." Dylan could hear them whispering through the paper-thin walls.

"Ask him who he is."

"Who be ya?" The rattle of the gruff voice almost made the panels of the door shudder.

"I came to talk to Mrs. Mathias about her son," said Dylan, trying to make his voice mellow and calm.

"Ain't got no son," responded the female voice despondently. "He be dead more 'n two years."

"Ma'am, can you open the door so we can talk?"

"You be from the law?"

"No, Ma'am. Your son works for me. I'd like to talk about what a fine son you have."

"Ain't my son. He be no good from his growin' up. He be dead in prison, I s'pose."

Dylan chatted through the door for a few moments; then the door swung open, and he gazed into the black eyes of a shriveled and stooped lady draped in a long thin gown.

It was late Sunday afternoon when Clarissa Williams Mathias and her man stepped from the limousine Dylan had hired. She stood up straight in her new wardrobe and clung to the arm of her man dressed in a sparkling new shirt, pants, and boots. She was nervous when Dylan took her arm and seated her at a table at the front of the hall that was set up for the occasion. A palpable vacuum hung over the empty chair beside her.

The hall was filled with ladies and gentlemen adorned with nametags from the bank. There were dignitaries from the city and people from the press.

Mr. Beckett was seated beside Jim Garber whose smile shone as he came to his feet. He raised his hands above his head and began clapping furiously.

"Mama?" Haydn asked stepping from behind the velvet curtain and quietly placing his huge hand on her shoulder.

Clarissa laid her wrinkled hand on his and wept.

Flash bulbs sent starbursts from the crowd, which was on its collective feet cheering and clapping.

Haydn lifted his mother to her feet and placed her hand on his arm. Together they disappeared through the curtain at the back of the stage.

After speeches and cheering for a man who refused to appear before them, Dylan searched and found Haydn with his mama nestled under his arm sitting on a loveseat in a darkened dressing room backstage. Snuggled under his other arm sat a dark-haired girl. In her hand she held the gnarled hand of the man she had longed to meet. She ran her hand along the dark skin of his massive arm. She looked up at the age-wrinkled golden skin of a mother whose son had returned from the dead.

"Angels do come in many wrappers," Gail said, "and your son's is lily white."

CPSIA information can be obtained at www.ICGtesting.com
Printed in the USA
LVOW10s1114090216

474344LV00017B/169/P